DREAMS REALLY
DO COME TRUE

Dreams Really Do Come True

by

John Entwistle

WORDS by DESIGN

Produced in association with

WORDS by DESIGN

www.wordsbydesign.co.uk
ISBN: 978-1-4709-6169-5

By the same author

Bolton Born and Bred

INTRODUCTION

My name is Sarah West, I am a freelance reporter, or at least was until early in the year 2000. I was at a press conference where Sir Alan Brown was promoting organic foodstuffs. The room was packed, heavy with smoke and everyone there wanted to ask a question.

I was finding it very hard just to get a question in when a note was pushed into my hand. "Sir Alan will see you after this conference." When we met he knew all about me – including that I had a first-class degree at Oxford in English and Philosophy. "I want someone to write my biography," he said, "are you interested?" Of course I was interested. Journalism was not paying off for me and I had considered packing it in. "No doubt you will wish to get to know me, and I you, before we make a contract," he added. "Come and spend a week with me and see what happens." And so I became his biographer at the age of 31 years.

CHAPTER 1

Alan Brown was born in the north east of England in a small town just outside Sunderland. It was April 16th 1954. England was only just coming out of rationing, although things were gradually beginning to improve. For Alan's parents, George and Gilly, life was still very hard. George was a small but well built man, strong as an ox. He was a proud man, wearing his bowler hat on a Sunday looking a million dollars. Gilly was a real mother who looked after her family. George came first in her life, but her children were a close second. She was born in 1916 and when Alan was born she was a good-looking woman. As a farmer's daughter, she had been brought up on a farm where she had to work hard, even as a young girl. Between them they raised a lovely family. Alan's older brother Jim was nearly 16 when Alan was born. His brother Charles was born in 1956 and sister, Alison, in 1958.

The family were very poor. George had been in the forces during the war and on demob had managed to find a job in the pit, his old pre-war job. He had married his childhood sweetheart Gilly and their first son Jimmy was already 16 when Alan was born and looking forward to the day when he would go down the pit.

As Alan grew up he was fascinated by mechanical things. He was always pulling things to pieces and putting them back together again. His father knew that Alan had a good brain and tried to stimulate the boy by trips to Sunderland to see the ships being built, very occasionally taking them as far as Newcastle. Mother would say, "You are putting ideas in the boy's head. You know he will have to go down the pit." But George knew better – somehow his Alan would be a great engineer, he just knew it. Alan would come home from these trips and dream that he would build ships just like the ones he had seen.

At 16 Alan and his father were invited into the headmaster's study. "Your boy is very talented with a good brain. He should go to university." George replied, "I know and have known for years that Alan has a good brain, but how can we get him to university with no money?" The headmaster pointed out that it was possible with good exam results to possibly get a sponsor, and gave them a list of companies in the area that had sponsored boys through university. The company that sprang out was Duxfords, a large ship builder in Sunderland, the one where Alan used to go as a child to watch the ships being launched. "I will give you a letter of introduction and recommendation to send with your own letter," the headmaster added.

With much labour, argument and discussion, the whole family wrote the letter. Alan posted the letter with great expectations. There was no reply that week, nor the following week – in fact it was five weeks after he had sent the letter that he received a reply. An interview was granted and he was to attend the following week. Alan couldn't sleep and neither could George, and the week before the interview went so slowly. Then the day arrived. Alan wore his best Sunday clothes – jacket and pressed trousers with a blue shirt. He knew exactly where to go by tram and then bus, and finally he stood outside the gates, just where he and his father had stood many times over the last years.

He had his letter. He was directed to the offices to be interviewed by a kindly middle aged gentleman, a Mr Brooks, who turned out had been a coal miner, one of the Bevan Boys in 1943. At the time the war effort was at its height it was discovered that the country was desperately short of coal. Ernest Bevan, the Minister of Labour, announced that one in ten of the new conscripts would have to work down the mines.

Mr Brooks made Alan welcome, asked him a number of questions and eventually showed him around some of the shipyard. "Subject to your 'A'-level results, we will offer you a sponsorship through university for mechanical engineering." He continued, "The company will pay all university costs, accommodation and books. You will only have to find money for food and clothing. I suggest you look at Sheffield University." Alan was over the moon. He couldn't wait to tell the rest of the family.

When he got home his dad was so delighted that he took the whole family out to celebrate with a fish and chip meal. The rest of the family were of course delighted and even Jimmy congratulated him. Alan realised that he had to get good results for his 'A'-levels in two year's time. He also realised that he had to earn money during this time for the family, so he had to get a part-time evening job. It had been quite a long day, but he still got no sleep thinking and dreaming of his future.

Over the next two years he worked hard. He was taking maths, physics and economics. He loved it all. The studying was no problem and he had managed to get a fill-in job at a small engineering workshop. At first he swept the floors, made tea for the other men and gradually made himself useful. Gradually the men accepted him, showed him various jobs they were doing, and he learnt to operate the lathes and milling machines. He loved the engineering and he really enjoyed everything he was doing at school as well.

The two years passed very quickly and the exams came and went. Waiting for the results was horrendous. Eventually they came through – three 'As', a wonderful result. The headmaster congratulated him and suggested he ring Mr Brooks at the shipyard.

CHAPTER 2

Alan started at Sheffield University on 26th September 1972. It was a totally new world — friends to be made, new clothes to wear, and life on the campus for those first few days was hectic. He was in the halls of residence a room to himself — that was a first. That first weekend he tramped around Sheffield trying to find a part-time job. He was lucky to find a small general store experimenting in opening on Sundays. Alan was offered work on Saturday and Sunday. It was a different type of work to what he had previously done, meeting people and selling to them. It was hard at times, but it paid for his food and clothes.

Three years passed quickly. In his last year it happened. He was rushing to a lecture one day when he saw her. She had black hair and a figure to die for. Alan fell in love. It took all of five seconds. Who was she? What was her name? How should he approach her? He had been out with girls but had never had a girlfriend. What should he do? Alan followed her at a safe distance. She went into the engineering school and into the same lecture that he was attending, one of general interest for all engineering students. Alan discovered that she was a fresher, new to the university that year. During the lecture any final year students were invited for comments. Alan stood up. He was invited on to the stage and was able to give himself good credit from what he said about the course, that university was good, and managing get a few laughs along the way.

As everyone was leaving the lecture theatre he caught up with the girl. "Excuse me," he asked, "are you doing engineering?"

"Yes," she replied.

"Is this your first year?"

"Yes".

Alan asked, "Would you like any of my lecture books? I am in my final year."

"Yes," she replied, "I would."

"I'll bring some tomorrow. Let's meet in the refectory. What time would suit?"

"Oh twelve noon."

"My name is Alan, what's yours?"

"Susan."

"Right, see you tomorrow."

Alan spent the night thinking about what he could say to Susan, but it was no use planning – he just had to rely on immediate reaction. They met up at twelve o'clock. Susan was already there when he walked in. She was delighted with the books and Alan went to get two coffees. Susan's parents lived in Lincoln and her father had his own printing business. She had always wanted to be an engineer. Susan was obviously impressed with Alan, his contribution to the lecture and he was obviously clever. They had lunch together and agreed to meet up the following week. Matters could not have gone better from Alan's point of view. Susan and Alan continued to meet up, and he took her out to the cinema several times. However, it made him more determined than ever to do well in his degree, despite the distraction.

Just before the break for Christmas, Susan invited Alan to go to her parents' house for the weekend. It was her brother Stephen's 21st birthday party. They had a fabulous party at a restaurant with about 30 people. Alan got on with her parents and met Stephen's friends, most of whom were at university. Susan's house was a lovely detached home with a large garden, and even her mother and brother had their own cars. Stephen was at Edinburgh University reading obscure Philosophy. When Alan went home for Christmas the contrast between where he lived and Susan's home was enormous.

Although it made him quite depressed, they all had a good Christmas and he bought small presents for all the family. He had given Susan a small locket she had bought Alan a scarf.

Over the rest of the university year his friendship with Susan developed and Alan did very well in his final exams getting his forecast 'first'. His friendship with Susan continued and they agreed that they would continue seeing each other, Susan still being at the university for another two years.

Alan had a short holiday and joined Duxfords Shipyard in August 1975. The company was huge, having been formed in 1841. They had built hundreds of ships and were also known worldwide for their diesel engines. Alan started in the design department and quickly found his way around. He had arrived at a good time – new ideas abounded and the design of ships was changing fast.

The company had had a major investment the previous year as Duxfords had been taken over in 1973 and become part of Sunderland Ship Builders Ltd. The year that Alan joined them they became the largest enclosed shipyard in the world. Although the company had had difficult times, it was now riding the crest of the wave – eight Bank Line vessels were constructed between 1976 and 1978. So Alan had joined at a good time, and after several months learning in each department of the company, he became a junior manager in the Development Design Office.

Alan threw himself into the job. He enjoyed every minute, was always at work early and usually the last person to leave. The whole work stretched his imagination and his abilities. Sunderland to Sheffield was over 100 miles, so he had agreed with Susan to try and see her every two months or so. Of course they wrote to each other several times a week, and so the romance continued at a distance. Alan was convinced that Susan was the girl for him, but he felt that Susan's feelings were not as strong as his. However, when they met up they had wonderful times and were able to spend all Saturday and most of Sunday together.

On one of their weekends together, Alan decided to take Susan to Whitby, south of Sunderland and right on the coast. He had once been as a child and had loved it – an aunt had taken him for a day out and they had had a fantastic time. He had always wanted to go back there and this was the opportunity. Susan had travelled up from Sheffield especially to see him and as Alan had recently passed his driving test he wanted to show off a little to Susan. He hired a car and off they drove to Whitby.

Alan and Susan took a large picnic lunch with them, and sat right up on the hill overlooking the sea. It was a wonderful view and Alan started dreaming. He said to Susan, "You know one day I'm going to own a shipyard, not work in one, and I'm going to have a big house overlooking the sea, just like this. I shall have a sea-going yacht and a plane, a light aircraft that I can fly myself. I'm going to have a Bentley car."
Susan said, "How are you going to get all these things?"
Alan said, "Oh, you wait and see, I'll get them all."
They had a wonderful day out and it was late when they got back to Alan's digs.

Back at the shipyard his main task was to try and introduce the wonderful new production facilities into the ship design. The new yard was a ship factory, unlike anything that had previously been built, with facilities and resources radiating from the assembly dock. Alan was totally absorbed in his work and he became well recognised for his contribution. His salary improved and the future looked good. He had moved his digs to better more comfortable accommodation. Life was good and he was enjoying it.

CHAPTER 3

Alan's father and eldest brother Jimmy were both involved in a car accident and both were killed. The good times did not last.

His poor mother was distraught and suddenly Alan became the head of the family and the main breadwinner. Charles, his younger brother, finished university, again as an engineer, and his sister Alison was just starting at university. She was a clever girl and wanted to become a veterinary surgeon. Although Alison had managed to get a scholarship to the Royal Veterinary College in London, the problem was now money.

Alan decided that the first thing he must do would be to move back into the family home. He managed to get Charles a job at the shipyard and was determined that sister Alison should stay at university. It was a long five-year course to train as a veterinary surgeon, but she dearly wanted to do this and Alan felt that she would make a first-class vet.

The police investigation into the car accident proved conclusively that for some reason the truck going in the opposite direction with which they collided had veered across the road. It was therefore not George and Jimmy's fault in any way. The driver of the truck unfortunately died in the accident, and it had taken many hours to separate the two vehicles and reclaim the bodies. Of course compensation came to mind, and a claim was made through their insurance company.

The claim went on and on. Eventually two-and-a-half years later they were awarded full compensation and paid £600,000. Such a large amount of money would certainly keep Alan's mother for the rest of her life. It also helped with Alison's education, so from a financial point of view they were now fairly well placed.

Charles was thoroughly enjoying his work at the shipyard, again in the engineering production department, and he was courting a young lady whom he hoped soon to marry. Despite all the concerns and worries for the family, Alan progressed in his job and became senior manager in charge of design at the age of 26. He was now earning a worthwhile salary and was thoroughly enjoying the work. He had of course kept contact with Susan who had decided on leaving university to spend a year or two in East Africa, helping the developing world with engineering problems.

However, the years had passed and Susan was still out of the country. One of the secretaries at the shipyard had been making eyes at Alan for some time now. Doreen was an attractive 22-year-old, and eventually Alan succumbed and took her out. They had a really excellent evening and she was very friendly and affectionate. Surprisingly to Alan, she was also quite intelligent and they got on well. One thing led to another, and as the months went by, Doreen announced she was pregnant. Alan of course did the only honest thing that he could and asked her to marry him, and the wedding was to be held within five weeks. It was 1972. Alan wrote to Susan and told her that he was to be married to Doreen in the middle of June. He had a brief reply from Susan wishing him well.

Susanne was born two days before Christmas. She was a beautiful little baby and Alan admitted he was over the moon with her. Bill was born just 18 months later and so they had a real family. They had moved to the outskirts of Sunderland and everything appeared to be going well. Doreen resumed her job in the middle of 1980, and grandmother Gilly was in her element looking after the babies and helping around the house. She had bought a small car, and much to everyone's surprise, turned out to be a good driver.

11

CHAPTER 4

During the mid and late 1970s, Alan had found himself at the forefront of the introduction of computer-aided techniques in ship building. He took to the new disciplines like a duck to water, and became a leading light in the promotion of electronic controls and mini-computer installations into shipyard building. In 1979 he decided after a great deal of thought that he would like to start his own business in this field of development. He had started with Duxfords in 1975. In order to pay back his sponsorship he had agreed to work for them for a minimum of three years. He had worked for them now for six years, and whilst they were reluctant to let him go, they recognised that they could not hold him forever. The dream he had had of starting his own company became a reality.

Initially Alan worked from home, Doreen typing the letters at night to various shipyards and organisations around the country. Alan was well recognised in the field and very quickly began to gain contracts. He opened a small office on the outskirts of Sunderland, taking on two people that had previously worked at Duxfords. The business developed fast and furiously. Profit margins were good, and the clients absolutely delighted with the developments that could be made. Alan travelled fairly extensively across Europe getting contracts almost wherever he went – Italy, France and Holland. By 1980 he was employing twelve people. His second-in-charge, David Agapath, had come from Russia and was extremely competent in computer languages. The company was called ABDS Ltd, the initials of his family.

Although David was very capable of running the company from day-to-day, all the customers still wanted Alan to do their work, and try as he did to develop his team, the customers were not content unless Alan dealt with them.

Nevertheless, Alan decided to take an extended holiday for three weeks. Alan and Doreen took their children on wonderful holidays by the seaside, and now as Bill was four-years-old and Suzanne six, Alan and Doreen took them abroad. They travelled to France and down to the south west of the country where the weather was gorgeous and the family learnt to sail. They visited the 'Pilladoon', a huge mountain of sand where they climbed to the top and then rolled all the way down. They really had a wonderful time.

They took two days driving home, enjoying the scenery, and they stopped off on the Sunday morning in Paris, where they spent a few hours driving round when there was little traffic. Crossing the Channel on the ferry was exciting for the children and the weather was perfect. Completing the journey back up north, Alan was really ecstatic – they had really had a lovely holiday, they were a family, and Alan began to realise, probably for the first time, that he was lucky to have married Doreen.

They repeated this trip to France the following year and then the next year they went to Italy. A few years later they went on safari to South Africa – that really was a wonderful trip spending a full week in the Kruger Park. The whole family loved the animals and Bill counted 46 bird species he had seen.

Everything seemed to be progressing beautifully. The company was developing slowly and was profitable, so Alan and Doreen had moved into a larger house, again on the outskirts of Sunderland. It was a detached property with four bedrooms and a large kitchen (which they modernised), dining room, study and garage. The back garden was a good size and Alan had a summer house built which the children used as a playroom. Suzanne was a lovely girl, growing up and developing, very intelligent and loving school. Bill was a bit more difficult, but then Doreen said that boys were. However, Bill did well at school and they had no real worries on that account. Four years later Suzanne went to Sheffield University, following in her father's footsteps, and Bill was heading in the university direction as well. Alan's dreams seemed to be coming true.

CHAPTER 5

One Friday night in May 1997 Doreen announced that she was going off in the morning for a week's holiday with some of her girlfriends. Whilst Alan was surprised as Doreen had never done this before, it had dawned on him that things had been quite strange between them during the last year or so. On reflection he felt that perhaps this was a good idea to get away from each other for a little while. He took his wife and friends to the airport and on the way home was quite melancholy.

When he arrived home, he made himself a cup of tea and wondered what to do. By lunch time he was really quite bored and pondered whether to go to the office or not. He watched the football on television but it wasn't very exciting, and by four o'clock he was really quite miserable. "I could do with a holiday as well," he said to himself. "David can run the firm, its summertime and we're a bit quiet. I can't see that there are any problems. I have always wanted to go to Cornwall, I am going to go."

So he rang David and told him that he was going away for the week. He threw a few clothes in a case, jumped in his Jaguar and off he went. It was around about ten o'clock at night when he got to the south of Cornwall, not knowing exactly where he was heading. It was getting dark, he was tired and very hungry. He pulled in at a petrol station and filled up and asked the attendant if he could recommend a bed and breakfast place. "Yes," he replied, "go and see Molly who lives at No. 14 on Harbour Road in Eaton Stanton village, next turning on the left." So Alan went down to the village, knocked on number 14, one of the fishermen's cottages in a row of about 20, and eventually the door opened. He said he had been recommended the place for bed and breakfast. Molly scanned him up and down, saw the smart car parked outside and said, "Yes, I only do bed and breakfast, I don't do any other meals. Take your car round the back where there is room to park it."

As he went into the house it was surprisingly large, much larger than it looked from the outside. He was given the front room overlooking the dockside, but being shown his room Alan really started to feel very woozy. He really was not well. Molly asked if he had eaten at all that day. When Alan replied that he had not, Molly told him to wash and come down for some soup. So Alan had a hearty bowl of soup, bread and a cup of tea before he went off to bed with Molly's voice echoing in his ears, "Breakfast at nine o'clock."

Next morning Molly cooked the breakfast. Nine o'clock came and went and there was no sign of her guest. She went upstairs and knocked on the door. No response. Ten minutes later she went up again. This time she tentatively opened the door, but Alan was flat out in the bed. It transpired that Molly was the wife of a local fisherman who had had his own fishing boat. Sadly both he and the crew were lost in a storm six months previously. Molly had one child, a daughter named Barbara, who was eight years old. Before she was married Molly had been a nurse, a sister at the local hospital, and it was there that she had met Matt her husband when he had come in to have a broken arm repaired.

She looked at Alan in the bed and recognised that he was unconscious. She had thought that he was not well the night before. After Molly called him, James Leather the local doctor arrived at half-past ten, but Alan was still unconscious. He examined Alan and was a little worried but decided that he would be better not to be moved – Molly was a first-class nurse, so he felt that the man would be in good hands. He would call again in the afternoon to see how Alan was. Molly and Dr Leather decided between them to go through the man's pockets and bag where they found his home address and telephone number. Molly immediately rang, but there was no reply

Molly and the doctor discussed the man upstairs. Molly told James how Alan had arrived the previous night and said that he had not eaten anything. The doctor decided to leave Alan where he was and visit again in the middle of the day. He felt very confident that with Molly's nursing abilities Alan would come to no harm.

Early in the afternoon Alan started to come round. He couldn't remember where he was and at first was very confused, but Molly was able to reassure him and eventually Alan recovered his full consciousness. He ate more of Molly's delicious soup and started to feel a little bit better. When Dr Leather arrived he was fast asleep again, although the doctor realised that Alan had been totally exhausted and was now starting to recover in a normal way. That evening Alan started to apologise to Molly for being such a nuisance, but Molly would have none of it. In fact she was thinking how good it was to have something real to do, to look after a patient again. Alan explained that his wife was away on holiday and that there was no one at home, hence why there was no one they could contact at the moment. Molly told him not to worry – he could stay as long as wished and she would look after him.

Alan was recovering and getting better, but very, very slowly. The doctor insisted that he stayed in the bedroom, and although he was allowed to walk around, he mostly stayed in bed. Molly really looked after him, serving him the best of food even though he didn't eat that much.

At the beginning of the following week Alan rang his wife, but surprisingly she put the phone down on him. He made several calls with the same conclusion. Molly rang on his behalf, but again had the same treatment. At the end of the second week he wrote to Doreen to explain the circumstances and apologise for not being at home when she arrived back from holiday. He rang David Agapath to explain that he had been very ill and was stuck in Cornwall, probably for several more weeks. The foreman said everything was going fine, that he was having a daily conference with Doreen, and that Alan need not worry about any non-existent problems at the office.

From Alan's bedroom window he could see the old lighthouse, now disused, and he vowed that as soon as he was well enough he would try and visit it. He also conceived a gem of an idea. At first he wanted to convert the lighthouse into a beautiful home, which would really have been very excellent with views of the sea and the surrounding countryside. However, then the idea of using the lighthouse room at the top of the building came into his mind in a dream.

The idea was to develop a scanning machine which used two very powerful binocular type viewers. These would scan the horizon up to 25 miles from land in an arc some 50 miles wide. They would be able to register within the segment any ship or boat entering it, watch its movement, register its speed and exact direction and also be able to watch small boats leaving the shore line. It would calculate the number of the people on-board and whether that boat had made a rendezvous with any of the larger craft out at sea, and if anybody had entered or left the large boat. All this information would be recorded electronically on a computer. If anything appeared slightly unusual this information could be reported to the local customs.

The more Alan thought about his idea, the more the concept appealed to him. Perhaps he could put a stop to illegal immigrants entering the UK. Perhaps it could prevent drugs being landed.

In the midst of this planning, a few days later Alan received a letter from a solicitor who purported to be acting on behalf of his wife Doreen asking to initiate divorce proceedings. Alan was totally taken aback – this was totally unexpected. However, as he thought about it, he recalled that things had become strange with Doreen over the last year or so, and he wondered in fact whether she was seeing someone else.

Both the doctor and Molly advised him against going home at this stage of his recovery, or on any journey involving a long distance. He wrote back to the solicitor saying that due to his health he was unable to travel and could not therefore visit his wife, and that this information regarding a divorce had taken him completely by surprise. The solicitor replied by return, advising him to employ his own solicitor.

Alan decided to discuss this problem with his new friends, the doctor and with Molly. The doctor re-affirmed that Alan really was not in a fit state to travel. Although he was now allowing Alan to go out a little, it was only for a gentle walk. The doctor put Alan in touch with the local area solicitors, Lord, Lord and Fletcher. Alan explained the circumstances and Mr James Lord said that he would come and visit Alan.

The meeting took place the following Tuesday. The first question of course was whether Alan still wanted to remain married. Alan was gradually getting over the shock and came to realise in his mind that there was no point in continuing. The solicitor pointed out that he would probably need to split everything in two halves. The company of course was the problem – without selling it they could not liquidate the assets. After a two-hour meeting the solicitor agreed to act on Alan's behalf.

Alan wrote to his children, Suzanne and Bill, and told them what he knew. Unknown to Alan, they had already been prepared by Doreen and so blamed Alan for being the one who had created the upset. Alan tried his best to put things right with them, but he did not think they really believed him. Susanne was now at university and whilst upset about the divorce, seemed to cope really well with it, whereas Bill was only 16 and was struggling with his exams.

CHAPTER 6

Each day Alan walked down to the harbour. Eaton Stanton was typical of many fishing villages – picturesque, beautiful, and Alan wished he could stay here the rest of his life. He talked to the fishermen, and talked in fact to anybody who would talk back to him. He got to know most of the villagers. They all knew Molly of course, and knew that she had a boarder. Alan found that everyone he met was kind and friendly. The fishermen were struggling with the new European directive that had cut their fish take by nearly 50%. They now had ten fishing boats in the harbour, where previously it had been 20. The young people were leaving the village as there was very little work, and the one shipyard was down to just the owner and a lad of 16. It had been handed down generation to generation and had built the fishing boats for miles around for over 120 years.

Alan went along to the shipyard. It was of course very different from the huge Duxford yard that he had worked at nearly 20 years previously. Recently the yard had only been used for the repair of local fishing boats, but in the past it had been used for construction, usually up to 50 or 60 feet in length, with beams usually about one-third of the length, sometimes considerably wider. They were a very well established yard and the current owner, Charlie Brakewater, had run the company for nearly 50 years. The yard had been started by grandfather 'Big Charlie' in 1880. However, over the last 20 years, with the decline of the fishing industry, the yard had diminished. The slipway and the buildings were still there, but mostly in a derelict condition. It made Alan feel quite depressed that a once flourishing business in the ship building industry was now something of a derelict heap. Charlie was approaching 70 and was more than ready to retire.

The whole village of Eden Stanton and the other four nearby villages, two on either side (Great Mount, Little Mount, Coswin and Gronton) were all in a depressed state. The villages had developed on fishing – both inshore local fishing, with some of the vessels going further afield. The fish processing plant and fish market at Eden Stanton received fish from all of these villages and also from other nearby fish grounds. Yet the modern restriction on fishing decimated the small villages. Everything was really in decline. Shops were closing, people were leaving the area and houses were only being taken over as holiday homes.

Alan was feeling better and stronger by the day and loved walking down to the harbour, watching the boats coming and going, talking to the fishermen and local people. It was some three weeks later that he heard Molly saying that she was going to the meeting in the village hall. Alan knew Molly well enough to ask what the meeting was about. "Oh, it's between the farmers, fishermen and the whole village really," she replied. "They are trying to discuss what we can do about the future."
"Can I come?" asked Alan.
"Oh yes," said Molly, "it's open to anybody." So Alan went along to the meeting and sat towards the back of the crowded hall.

The chairman of the council gave an overview of the serious situation for the village and then asked for questions. There were a few, with one or two minor suggestions, but nothing that would make any real impact. Alan nervously put his hand up and the chairman asked him to stand.

Whilst Alan was known to perhaps most people in this room, he began tentatively. "I am very much a newcomer," he explained, "I became stranded in this village because I was extremely ill. I have found the people here quite wonderful, friendly, and helpful, and indeed I believe my life has been saved here. I would like very much to spend the rest of my life in this area. I have listened to what has been said this evening and for the last weeks I have spent most of my days near the harbour and around the village. I have had time to watch, to listen and to learn. Perhaps because of this I may have a very different approach to your problems."

He continued. "The centre of the problem is of course the fishing industry. There are currently ten fishing boats harboured and this we are told has to reduce to six. I don't believe it is any use making representations to the government or saying you are not going to do it, it is inevitable."

There was a bit of a stirring in the audience, but Alan went on. "I have in mind to suggest that a limited company is formed of the ten owners of those boats in order that you may act in unison. I believe it is inevitable that the two oldest vessels have to be scrapped. Two others can be converted into passenger vessels for sightseeing using grant aid money from the government. You have the most wonderful coastline with a lot of wildlife, dolphins, seals and birds. People are always anxious on holiday to do something. This local attraction I believe would be a large success. This will bring people to the village, hopefully regenerating shops and bringing immediate work to the shipyard with the conversions. More grant aid would be needed to create a suitable car park outside the village, with some form of bus transport perhaps for the elderly. Don't forget souvenir shops. The sands on the west side of the village are really gorgeous, and the walks around the area are really fantastic. I do believe you have an opportunity and you have to be radical in your thinking. Thank you for listening to me."

Then Alan sat down. There were no further questions and the meeting was soon closed and everyone departed. When they arrived home Molly told him, "I think what you said was wonderful! I think something may come of it."

A few days later the chairman of the village committee, Ray Crossley, came to see him. He asked Alan if he would allow his name to be put forward to be co-opted onto the committee to talk about the regeneration of the village. Alan replied that he would be delighted to do anything he could.

CHAPTER 7

Alan knew he was getting involved in the area. He also knew that with his divorce proceeding, he would no longer have any ties with the north east. He felt that this was now his home. He went to see the Lord of the Manor, Lord Copperfield, who owned most of the land in the area, including the disused lighthouse which was situated on Home Farm. Alan asked him if he would consider selling the lighthouse. "Definitely not," was Lord Copperfield's reply. "You can buy the whole bloody farm if you wish," he explained, "but not just the lighthouse." He was rather brusque and did not make Alan feel at all comfortable or welcome. There was no way that Alan could buy the whole 600 acre farm worth probably £3.5 million. He had nothing like that sort of money and never would have, so he would have to think again.

A few weeks later Alan travelled up to Sunderland for the hearing of the divorce. He went with his solicitor, James Lord, who drove the whole distance. The solicitor advised him to say little and leave the talking to the lawyers. This he did, and in fact neither he nor his wife Doreen said anything. An agreement on all the money issues was made – 50% to each. Alan went to the house listless, collected as much as he could of his personal possessions – his clothes and suits, and a few odds and ends that they could carry with them. There was no particular furniture that he wanted and really that was it. He arranged to put into storage locally his books and some other personal items. He tried unsuccessfully to speak to Doreen and neither of his children were there.

They returned to Eden Stanton very late and tired, and Alan thanked the solicitor for his help. On Saturday morning he received the confirmation from the court that everything had been decided and his marriage was over. Alan felt really quite miserable and very depressed. He wandered off down to the docks, ending up at the Post Office where he saw one of the villagers buying some lottery tickets. He had never bought a lottery ticket in his life and Alan asked the man to show him how to do it. Feeling in his pocket, Alan had £100 and he blew the whole lot on lottery tickets.

That night Molly was watching television. Molly always watched the Lottery results on Saturday evenings as she always bought a £1 ticket. Alan of course had a lot more interest but had decided that he had no chance of winning anyway. Somehow the mood he was in had caused him to spend all that money on those tickets.

Up came the results. Perhaps that was one of his numbers – or was it? He dashed upstairs to check the numbers. Sure enough it was one of his numbers – it couldn't be, what should he do? He kept all the tickets together in his pocket and slept with them under his pillow.

In the morning he rang the lottery company who told him that someone would come to verify his winnings. They asked if he would come up to London to receive the winnings if it was confirmed.

The next morning someone from the Lottery arrived on his doorstep, showed his credentials and Alan produced the ticket. It was confirmed that this was indeed the winning ticket and Alan was given a note to that effect. Alan was ecstatic.

He told Molly but asked her not to tell anybody else – not at the moment anyway. He had won over £25 million pounds – to be precise, £25,431,562. Alan could not sleep that night as he kept pondering what to do with his life. It wasn't just the money – it was his entire life. Molly had said that of course he could stay as long as he wished, as long as he paid the rent. He had already reached an agreement with Molly for all the extra time and food and everything that had been expended on him while he had been ill. Did he really want to spend the rest of his life in this area and put down his roots? What would he do?

His ideas on the shipping surveillance system that he had dreamed of became a real possibility. He would have to employ people to develop the idea. He had always fancied buying a yacht as well. Now he had the money, the opportunity and of course the place to keep it in the harbour.

That weekend he went up to London to receive the monies. He had asked Molly to go with him, but she said she would rather not. So he went by himself and was wined and dined at the Ritz. He drove back to Cornwall totally refreshed.

The Lord of the Manor, Lord Copperfield, was now a lot more receptive to his idea and agreed to sell Home Farm for £3.5 million. Alan made an appointment to see James Lord, his solicitor. He had always got on well with James, and they had become good friends. James was most surprised to see Alan again, and even more surprised when Alan said, "I have something to tell you. Please keep it to yourself. I have won 25 million pounds on the lottery." James was most pleased for Alan. "What will you do with the money?" he asked. Alan told him of his decision to stay in Eaton Stanton and his discussion with Lord Copperfield. Over the next few days James looked carefully at the deeds which were old and complex. There were no real problems relating to public access, so Alan decided to go ahead and buy it.

He went again to see Lord Copperfield. "Do you really want to sell Home Farm?" he asked. "I want 3.5 million," the Lord of the Manor replied. "That is rather overpriced," said Alan. "Well, if you want it, you will have to pay." Alan offered three million as his final offer. With that he shook hands and left. Three days later Lord Copperfield contacted his solicitors and agreed three million. He obviously needed the money.

Alan went to see the farm manager and told him that as far as he was concerned nothing would change. When things had settled Alan would consult him about how they were to develop. Judd Court seemed an affable sort of guy, and he was about Alan's age. His children had grown up and left home, but his wife Elle invited him in for a tea of homemade scones and the usual Cornish cream.

The first fine day that followed Alan walked from the main road across to his lighthouse. It was 2½ miles from the road, much further than he had thought. However, it was a lovely day and he enjoyed the walk. He had a key to the lighthouse, so he gingerly went inside, only just managing to open the door on its rusty hinges. It was just as expected – derelict and dirty, but salvageable. The stone steps were still perfect and the fabric of the building fine. Alan had a quick look round then left locking the door carefully behind him.

As he went back to the road he crossed the field diagonally to take a short cut. About halfway across the field stumbled over some stones. Looking around him they weren't just in any odd pattern – they appeared to be the foundations of what was once a large house or a castle, or something like that. He continued on his way, but that night an idea struck him – to use the lighthouse for the development of his idea, and then build a new house on the foundations with gorgeous views overlooking the sea and the lighthouse some distance away. Alan needed an architect.

That night in his sleep Alan had a dream. He dreamt that if he were to go to London and visit the Embankment, where all the down-and-outs were gathered at night, if he were to ask for 'Josh the architect', then on the third consecutive night he would find him. What a silly dream, Alan thought, but he remembered it and it kept turning around in his head.

Alan decided to go to the Southampton Boat Show in September. He had never been to a boat show before and was enthralled by all the vessels, including the huge ones which of course he could now afford. He went out on the water on a 45ft boat which was beautifully finished and which he was very seriously inclined to buy. A young man from the north east called Gerald Birch took Alan out in the boat, and the two of them got on famously. Gerald was a well qualified yacht designer and had spent most of the time since leaving university at a French shipbuilders, designing yachts for the wealthy. Alan was impressed by him and his ideas. Gerald had come back to England because he was about to get married to his longstanding girlfriend, a doctor. He had taken this temporary job during the exhibition but didn't have a permanent job to go to. Alan made a suggestion. "I have an idea. Would you be interested in being a part-owner of a shipyard designing boats and building them?" "Of course I would," Gerald replied. "Well come and see me next weekend, with your girlfriend, and let's talk about it. Let's not make any decisions, but talk about it." So it was agreed they would arrive on the Friday evening and spend the weekend with Alan. Alan decided to put off the purchase of the yacht for the moment.

The following weekend Gerald Birch and his fiancée, Jane, came down to Eden Stanton. Alan took them out to the local pub for lunch and decided that it would be fair to tell the couple about his own past – his experience, his qualification, his divorce and winning the lottery. They then visited the shipyard. He had asked Charlie to take them round and they spent nearly three hours looking over the whole yard. Charlie was keen to sell everything as the downturn in business had proved too much and had nearly brought him to his knees. The cost was relatively small – there was no goodwill business really, no employees, and it would have to be started from scratch.

Alan had given it a great deal of thought and he suggested to Gerald that he would offer him a 20% share in the yard, with a minimum contract of five years, but most of his earnings would come from the profitability of the yard. Gerald was very enthusiastic. He would need a production manager and some designs.

Alan also suggested a project – he would like to develop a yacht of about 60ft, with a speed of up to 65 knots. He thought that this would be obtained by placing retractable wings on the hull so that the yacht could rise above the water level, reducing the friction of the water over the hull. As for the shipyard, they could restart it quite quickly to convert the fishing boats into passenger-carrying vessels. It was not just the two boats from Eden Stanton, but a number of villages around and about felt they could use the same type of conversion. This would allow time for Gerald to design the yacht.

Jane was a little sceptical about whether the whole thing could be made to work. However, Gerald seemed enthusiastic and Alan suggested that they went away for a couple of weeks and then meet up again. Gerald said that there was a fairly large conference the following week in London for the European yacht building fraternity and invited Alan to attend with him. Alan had been waiting for an excuse to go up to London for sometime, remembering of course his dream of Josh the architect.

CHAPTER 8

Alan set out early on the Tuesday morning and drove up to London. Again he had booked the Ritz on Piccadilly which seemed to have become his regular hotel and he was becoming known there. As he drove up the porter welcomed him and his car was whisked away to the garage, his luggage to his room. After a light tea Alan had a word with the porter on his way out. He told him he was looking for a friend of his who was now down-and-out and believed was living on the Embankment. He wondered whether, if Alan was able to find him, perhaps the porter could find a back-way into the hotel as he may be embarrassed to bring his friend in through the front. The porter was understanding and offered Alan a number to ring should he find the man – he would wait at the side of the hotel, take them up through a service lift and book a back room for the man.

Alan thanked the porter and started walking towards the Victoria Embankment. It was about half a mile's walk and he enjoyed the autumn air of a dry pleasant evening. He started at one end of the Embankment and almost immediately came upon a number of down-and-outs. Rather nervously he asked whether anyone knew 'Josh the architect'. However, nobody did, and Alan moved onto the next gathering of people and asked the same question. He spent about two hours going up and down The Embankment, but with no joy, so he walked back to his hotel.

The next day was the conference so he met up with Gerald and they went in together. There were a number of eminent speakers. One in particular, a well -known yacht designer, said that he felt yacht design needed to have a much more radical approach and went on with some technical explanations which went over Alan's head. Gerald invited Alan out for dinner, but he was anxious to get back on his search on the Embankment so declined, saying that he had a prior engagement. He returned to the hotel, had a light snack in his room, and at around eight o'clock set out again to look for Josh. Once again, although he travelled much further, he was still unsuccessful. He got back to the hotel a little weary, but slept like a log.

Next morning he had a hearty breakfast. The hotel was really superb and the service fantastic. Afterwards he walked down Regent Street looking for a little present for Molly – she would definitely not accept any of his winnings from the Lottery, and he felt very indebted to her for all the effort she had put in looking after him and nursing him back to health. He found a small old-fashioned pendant, which he felt Molly would appreciate. With this in his pocket he couldn't wait for the evening to come – it was the third evening of his search for Josh.

Again, after a light meal in his room, he set out full of anticipation, whilst realising that the whole thing was really absolutely stupid and thinking that he must be mad. On the Embankment he retraced his steps of the first night. Nobody had heard of Josh, so he turned and came all the way back. Finally he was about to pack in for the evening when somebody asked, "You looking for 'Josh the architect'?" Alan replied, "Yes." "Oh, he's over there," and he pointed to a tall black man with a huge beard.

Alan felt a little scared, but he walked over and he asked, "Are you Josh the architect?" "Yes," said Josh. Alan explained that he was looking for an architect and that he had a wonderful piece of land with great views. He felt that Josh was the man to design the building. Josh had been living rough for three years ever since his wife had walked out on him. He had been quite a prominent architect in his home town of Leeds, but he was totally devastated and his life had been turned upside down when his wife went. Josh had packed his job in and moved to London and lived rough ever since. He was not looking forward to another winter as The Embankment was cold and damp and he was coming up to 36 years of age.

Alan offered, "Fancy fish and chips? I'm starving." "Ok," said Josh. So they walked a bit further along to a fish and chip van and Alan bought them both a meal. Josh enquired how he had come to know his name and where he was from. Rather embarrassingly Alan told him about his dream. "I really can't believe that it has worked out – the dream said that on the third consecutive night that I looked along this Embankment and asked for 'Josh the architect', I would find you. You are the exact person I am looking for. You must think that I am totally mad! But here I am and here you are – it must be fate or something." Josh thought and said, "I'm going to take a chance on you."

Alan got his phone out and rang the porter. "I'm on my way, can you fix the room?" On arriving at the hotel they went round the side and the porter was waiting for them. They went straight into a service lift and the porter showed them to a room on the same floor as Alan. "Thank you," said Alan, "can you organise for a barber at say 7.30 am tomorrow, and for a gentleman from Saville Row to measure my friend up for some clothes?" "Yes of course sir," the porter replied.

Alan followed Josh into the room. It was a small room by the standards of the Ritz, but nevertheless a very comfortable room, with a double bed and the most wonderful bathroom. Josh was much bemused, but was looking forward to a night in that bed. Alan suggested that he really ought to have a very good bath, perhaps more than one, before he got into the clean bed. In his own room Alan could not sleep for quite a while – life was crazy.

The next morning they both had breakfast in their rooms at 7.30 am. The barber arrived. "Shave it all off, shave the whole beard off and cut my hair back," said Josh. He had had a superb night's rest, despite not being used to the comfort, and he had eaten an enormous breakfast. Shortly after the barber had finished Alan came in. "Wow," he said, "what a difference – you are a very handsome man." "Be careful now," said Josh laughing. At nine o'clock the man from Saville Row arrived and Alan suggested that Josh would need a suit, a dress suit, shirt and ties, etc., as well as casual wear. The tailor asked Josh what sort of clothes he liked to wear. He ordered a couple of pairs of trousers and a light jacket, and also three pairs of shoes. It was now a matter of waiting until the suits were ready.

Whilst waiting for the new clothes, the two men played chess together, using a new chess set that Alan had bought the previous day. They also talked and Alan told Josh about his own divorce and what he had done in his life. Josh reciprocated – he had qualified as an architect in Leeds, and with help from his father had started a small architectural office. Life had progressed well, and five years later he had married. Whilst they did not have any children, Josh felt happily married and things were good. His wife was also an architect and worked in the business. Suddenly after five years of marriage she upped and left, filing for divorce and receiving half of the business. It was all too much and Josh left Leeds and went to London where he found himself on the streets.

Eventually the new clothes were delivered. Alan paid for them and they fitted Josh perfectly. He really looked a million dollars and now he had far better suits than Alan. Alan settled the account with the hotel, leaving an envelope for the porter with £50 to say thank you for his help the night before. They motored back to Cornwall.

Alan rang Molly and asked her to fix some accommodation for Josh in the nearby cottage. Both Josh and Alan were somewhat overcome by the fast turn of events and neither said a great deal during the drive down. They stopped for dinner and Josh, who had been drinking heavily over the last few years, made a decision that not another drop of alcohol would pass his lips, at least for the next twelve months. They arrived 'home' and Molly met them at the doorstep. Josh was to stay in the next house with Jeannette. Both men were pretty tired out with the momentous events of the last 24 hours.

The next morning Alan drove Josh out to the site of the proposed house. They walked from the road across to the foundations, then to the lighthouse and back again. Josh asked lots of questions and became enthusiastic about the site. Alan had some ideas of what he wanted for the house which he had jotted down. Over a light lunch they looked at Alan's sketch drawings and after a few more questions Josh said, "What a wonderful opportunity – I would like to accept your offer. I think it will take about 18 months to design and build – subject to getting planning permission in a reasonable time." Josh needed a temp to help with the measuring of the land, and they soon found that one of the fishermen's sons was ready to serve the purpose for a day or two. Alan had agreed to pay Josh a sum of £50,000 for the first year and also to pay for his accommodation in the village and transport.

Alan went to bed that night reflecting on what a truly unbelievable trip he had had. He had given the gold broach to Molly and she was over the moon. She told him if he continued to spend all his money like this he would soon have none – but she really liked the broach and gave him a big hug and kiss.

CHAPTER 9

Having his future home planned and underway, Alan turned his mind to his electronic horizon scanner, EHC for short. He knew the concept was pretty original and felt that with the lighthouse he had the facility to develop it. Standing on top of the cliff, the top of the lighthouse was nearly 200ft above the water. In order to develop it he required a mechanical genius and an electronic genius. Talking to Gerald over the next week, Alan mentioned that he was thinking of employing an electronic engineer, but he didn't tell Gerald what for. Gerald thought that such a person would be invaluable in the design of the yacht, particularly as they were considering electronic navigation and electronic control of the sails and rudder.

Alan felt that getting hold of these two people was going to be quite difficult – at least getting hold of the right two people as well as two people who could work together in close proximity for perhaps a year or more before achieving any real progress. He sought the advice of two or three recruitment agencies – each said they could find such people, so he put an advertisement with one of the agencies that he felt would best service his purpose. Alan sat back and waited for applications.

Gerald and Jean came to visit again at the weekend. Gerald was very keen to go into partnership with Alan and was ready to start straight away. Knowing his future, Alan and Gerald had discussions with Charlie Brakewater, the owner of the boatyard. They examined the deeds. The land was extensive, covering an area of some 40 acres on both sides of the river. The main sheds were on the land side, but the area between the river and the sea which ran out as a peninsular was completely forested. The forest had been planted by Charlie's grandfather and there were acres of beech, yew and oak trees. The covered part of the yard was a relatively small area in total, stretching over perhaps four-and-a-half acres with other areas such as the slipways and other assembly areas outside.

Charlie said that he would help with the recruitment of staff and suggested that they needed a production manager to kick off who would help with choosing the right staff. Another week went by with Alan and Gerald both enthusiastic. They agreed the price with Charlie – a quarter-of-a-million pounds. This included all the buildings, the slipways and the land on both sides of the river. It was a fair price. They had put a very small valuation on the goodwill, and a lot of the buildings were very derelict. So now it was full speed ahead with recruitment. Alan involved himself with finding the two highly qualified people for the EHS, and with the production manager of the shipyard. The whole procedure took about eight weeks, and in the end the three people were appointed.

John Stevens was a 30-year-old engineer who had a good degree from Bristol University and currently lived in Somerset, but was prepared to move. His wife was a nurse and could easily transfer. Alistair Roberts, an electronic wizard, was 28, again with a degree from Bristol. He was unmarried, but courting a young lady in Little Mount, one of the nearby villages. Finally for the production manager for the yard they hired Jim Caldwell, aged 36, who was well experienced in this size of yard and fairly local so had an idea of the sort of staff he was looking for.

Gerald and Jim got together to work out the sort of staffing they would immediately need for the ship repairs, but they were looking at something like 18 months before the shipyard got into real production on the yachts. They agreed to pass their findings to Alan before taking action. Gerald also met up with Alistair Roberts and they discussed briefly how electronics could be installed into a production yacht. He was very keen on the idea, and it certainly looked as though they would get on well together. They were all young, well qualified and an enthusiastic team.

Alan spent the best part of four days with John and Alistair. They discussed his ideas and how to go about them. They were concerned that any ideas that they developed could be copied relatively easily, so some time was spent on the value of taking out patents. Alan was tasked with taking it up with a patent agent over the next few weeks, and Alan felt that it really could go a lot further than the way he had described it. They got underway, firstly with the help of a couple of cleaners who cleaned out the lighthouse from top to bottom. Then they had it redecorated, restored the heating and the lighting, and they were fully installed within four weeks.

Alan of course had seen Josh the architect nearly every day and had spent some time making sure that he was content. Josh was delighted. He was really ready to get out of his cardboard box and to get back to the job he knew and loved. After a month or so he spent a whole day with Alan showing him the preliminary drawings of the house, as well as one or two of the external and internal features. Josh said that he had discussed the plans with the chief planning officer and had his acceptance. Now he had to do the detailed drawings and formally apply for planning permission.

Alan poured over the plans, spending hours thinking how it would work. Josh had certainly taken his original ideas and put them down in a concrete form. He had altered a few, but on the whole they were as Alan had imagined. It would be a beautiful place, a majestic building with a long half-a-mile drive leading from the road. Alan explained, "You will need to keep the driveway straight because I have an idea that this could be a landing strip for small aircraft. If things go well with the companies then I think this is a good possibility." The road of course had to be one of the first constructions to be made, as nothing could get onto the site until it was in place. The timing really could not be better – it was coming up to the end of November and Josh hoped that the plans would be ready and through the planning procedure by the end of March, giving them a flying start at the end of the bad weather. Josh had been looking at various builders around the area and had decided that he would have to go further afield to get the type of builder he wanted. Alan suggested that he should select at least three builders in order to get three competitive prices.

On the financial side, Alan's investments were bringing in over £1¼ million. So at the moment, in spite of employing all these key staff, he was still very fluid and his grand plans, for the moment anyway, were working out.

The site on which the house was to be built had a total of 120 acres. It was a good half-a-mile from the road to the house and beyond the house to the edge of the cliffs was a further half-a-mile. Alan's plan was to have a long straight drive from the road, aiming at just running slightly past the house, which would allow the road to be developed as a runway for light aircraft in future use. The lighthouse was of course right on the edge of the cliffs – it was itself about 120-130 feet high, and the cliffs at this point stood some 200ft above sea level. Below the cliffs at sea level, the large rocks in the sea had created a natural harbour and over the years the sea and wind had dug out a huge cavern into the rock face. The sea was on the south side of the site and the road on the north. On the west was a small river which separated the land from the next farm. On the east the land sloped away giving general access to the seashore and sandy beach. At the south east corner of the site was a huge lake approximately twelve acres in size.

The house was to be sited with the main rooms and windows pointing to the south east. By the standards of the whole estate it was not a large house, utilising about 10,000 sq ft altogether. There was to be a magnificent entrance hall with small columns on either side of the main door. Immediately inside to the right some toilets, on the left a cloakroom, and then through a second door into the great hall. This would be a magnificent hall and directly opposite the entrance to the hall a window stretching from wall to wall and from ceiling to floor. This would then look out onto a large patio.

In the plans the hall had a large fireplace on the left hand side wall in the middle designed to burn wood logs. Immediately on entering the hall you turned left through a doorway into the lounge with an Inglenook fireplace on the eastern wall. On the south facing aspect of the lounge was a large conservatory. The north facing window was bow-fronted.

Back to the hall, where the surprising element was that there was no staircase. Turning immediately right on entering the room lead through to a complex staircase or lift up to the first floor level. Back again in the hall beyond this secreted staircase was the opening to a passage-way. Immediately on the right was the dining room, again with a bow-fronted window. Further on in the hall was access to a large study with a bow-fronted window facing south, and door access to a cloakroom with toilet, washbasin and space for coats and boots and beyond that the library. Going back to the corridor and beyond the dining room was the butler's room, and immediately opposite on the other side of the corridor the butler's pantry and wine cellar. Further on down the corridor to the right was a large kitchen facing north and again with a bow-fronted window. On the left was the laundry, directly opposite the kitchen.

Upstairs on the first floor there were eight bedrooms, with the master suite on the far left of the house taking the morning sun and overlooking both the east garden and on the south aspect the view down across the gardens and lake to the sea. Next to the master bedroom were the principal guest room and four other guest rooms. There was also the butler's and cook's accommodation on this floor. All eight bedrooms were en-suite.

Whilst exposing the foundations of the house in order to plan the development, Josh discovered access to a tunnel. The access hole was about 30ft deep and bricked all the way down with steps going the whole distance. Reaching the bottom there was a tunnel, but at this point Josh decided that discretion was the better part of valour, and so he returned to the open air above. However, on telling Alan about this they decided to investigate further.

The pair did not want to divulge the knowledge of the tunnel to everybody, so they decided to investigate it themselves. They went down one morning, taking with them a length of rope, several large torches and a couple of spades. The tunnel started off very smooth. There was a sort of sandy gritty floor to the tunnel which was quite large with about 5ft headroom and 5ft in width, so they had no problem at all in walking, or rather stooping along the tunnel which progressed downwards at quite a rate. They were able to measure a pretty even 1ft fall for every 6ft travelled. It obviously led to the bottom of the cliffs. There were a couple of small rock slides, but otherwise the tunnel of 800yds in length was in near-perfect condition. It ended up with a very heavily bricked wall, so both Alan and Josh decided to leave that and retrace their steps and have a look from the sea. They had taken a compass with them and so were able to estimate approximately where the tunnel was likely to come out at the bottom of the cliffs. The tunnel was remarkably dry and whilst it smelt a bit musty, there was obviously air getting into the tunnel – probably from the sea end as there were no apparent ventilation shafts.

The following day Alan and Josh went down to the seashore. They had estimated where the tunnel came out correctly, at the head of the large cavern which had opened up from the sea end, creating a natural harbour for a small vessel. It had a quayside which ran straight out into the bay. The bay was naturally formed with huge rocks jutting out from the cliffs and standing clear in the water for some 50yds out into the sea. The tunnel entrance was well disguised and extremely well bricked up. The brickwork was obviously very old so it had been blocked for a considerable time and undoubtedly it had been used for smuggling on quite a grand scale.

The smuggling around this coastline had been prevalent, reaching a peak in the middle of the 18th century. At this particular site it was obviously a fairly grand affair. The quay was a natural one, formed out of the solid rock that protruded right from inside the cave right out into the water. At low tide there was nearly 15ft of water available so quite large ships could come in, moor up and off-load their goods. This could be done by smaller vessels inside the cave itself, and by larger vessels on the outside of the cave. Even in rough weather the bay was very well protected. Alan decided there and then that the access through the tunnel would be concealed within the house and possibly some use could be made of this at a later date.

Plans for the house were submitted to the local council for approval. Having discussed the matter with the principal planning officer, neither Alan nor Josh felt there would be any real problems getting the permission. Josh turned his mind to landscaping and designing the gardens. Alan wanted a large herd of deer to occupy the front of the house on the west side. They would be restrained from walking onto the driveway by an electric fence. South of the house was largely taken up with lawns, the large lake of course, which was very impressive, and trees which were to be planted to allow the views to be enhanced. A large kitchen garden was planned again on the south side of the house towards the western side.

CHAPTER 10

Alan left all the details of the house to Josh and moved his attention firstly to the new shipyard. He re-named it 'Cornwall Shipyards'. Having secured the order from the Eden Stanton village fisherman to convert two fishing vessels to passenger carrying craft (with substantial grant aid from the government), Alan set forth to the nearby villages of Great Mount, Little Mount, Coswin and Gronton. At each village he explained what they had done at Eaton Stanton. He was at pains to inform them that they would not compete successfully if they met the Eaton Stanton fishermen head-on – they had to find other types of development. Two of the villages opted to convert a couple of boats for pleasure fishing and again Alan got the job.

He went over to the north Devon and north Cornwall coasts and again picked up a few orders en-route. He was offering some good ideas and the government grant was making life much easier to help the fishermen change their boats from fishing to some other activity. Cornwall Shipyards was busy recruiting labour and they had enough work for over twelve months. Alan spent quite a lot of time with Gerald and they took on two other designers to get on with the fishing boat conversions. These of course had to be compliant with all the latest health and safety rules for passenger-carrying vessels.

Gradually Gerald was able to turn his mind to the yacht design. This was his primary task and he knew it. Alan was dogmatic about wanting a luxury fast cruiser – if somebody wanted to make an all-out racing vessel it would need to be stripped out of all the luxuries.

Alan felt that the money was with the luxury side. He also felt that the vessel should travel just as quickly under power as it did under sale. There was a lot of work for Gerald to get on with, but he was the sort of guy that knew what he wanted and worked very hard to achieve the ultimate aim.

Jim Caldwell, the production manager, had his hands full of work and was really proving to be a very good manager of men. Applicants for work at the yard were queuing up. The first boat converted for Eden Stanton was completed and handed over with great ceremony. It had taken just over three months to complete, and all trace of the fishing boat that used to be had disappeared. The outline and general look of the vessel was still there, but the whole of the interior, bridge and exterior decks were now lavishly completed for the general public. The publicity they received from the handover was national and even appeared on television news. It certainly generated more enquiries from all over the country and some from France as well. This conversion business was proving to be much bigger than Alan had initially expected and it was good business.

The local people were delighted that the business was bringing younger people back into the villages, creating an air of expectation and prosperity. People were even phoning the local tourist board hoping to book up accommodation either in Eden Stanton or close by. The bed and breakfast industry was booming, and the hotels were starting to fill up. One local shop in Eden Stanton, which had been empty for over twelve months, was bought up. The new owners turned it into a store selling ice creams, gifts, beach items etc. It was the first time in many years that a shop had opened in the village.

Gerald had produced his first overall plans of the new yacht. It really did look very impressive and Alan was delighted. They had to take on another young designer to assist Gerald with the work. Gerald was also concerned as to where they should build it – the shipyard was pretty full with conversion work and it wasn't the right sort of place to build a larger yacht. Alan agreed, so they decided to build a new covered shipyard and sail loft. They brought Josh into the conversation and put him in charge of the design of the new yard.

The depth of water was important, as of course these were keel boats requiring a much deeper draft than the in-shore fishing boats. Alan also asked John Stevens, the engineer working on the EHS, to cast his eye over the mechanics of the drive. John suggested that it may be worthwhile looking at a turbo type of propulsion – he was no expert in the area, but he felt that this might give them flexibility.

It was John who had the idea that perhaps the engine pods should be separate to the boat and anchored to the outside of the vessel – when not in use they could be trussed to the body of the boat and when in use lowered down to keep within the water line as the boat rose out of the water. Both Alan and Gerald felt this was an idea worth exploring.

Josh drew up the plan for the small covered yard which would only be used for yachts, and with a few small alterations this was put before the planning committee. Eventually it was agreed and the building went up very rapidly – it seemed to Alan almost overnight.

There were two elements to the new yacht. The hull and superstructure would both be moulded in fibreglass and fitted together with a moulded interior. Between the inside and outside skins would be water-tight compartments and also fuel and water tanks in the lower areas. Each fibreglass moulding was to be moulded by a subcontractor and the elements brought by road or sea to the shipyard for assembly. They envisaged that at a later stage they might develop their own fibreglass manufacturer on site. The fitting-out would be done at their own yard.

The design of the fibreglass superstructure and various other fibreglass components were of vital importance, incorporating the buoyancy of the vessel, the water tank and engine fuel tanks, and above all the watertight compartments. All these elements were held between the outer and inner skins. Gerald had had wide experience on this type of construction, but nevertheless he passed the whole lot over to John, a friend of his, who was involved in this type of work. After considerable discussions it was decided that, initially anyway, the fibreglass elements would be manufactured by John's company.

Developments were moving along quite quickly, and Alan found it all very exciting and extremely interesting. However, there were other irons in the fire, and Alan turned his attention to the developments of the EHS. John Stevens, the engineer he had taken on, was definitely the right man. He was full of ideas, full of enthusiasm and a very good engineer. He got on well with Alistair Roberts, the electronics wizard, and the two of them were making substantial progress – although of course there was nothing really to see at this stage of the game.

They had taken over the lighthouse which, when cleaned out both inside and out, had become a beautiful building and very desirable. Both John and Alistair were comfortable at working in the old lighthouse and in fact each day they travelled together from their homes just down the coast. They were both enjoying the location and were still enthusiastic about the proposition.

Alan had met the Chief Constable for Cornwall at a dinner and he had made a mental note that when the time was right he would invite the Chief Constable, the Head Coastguard and Head of Customs in the area to meet up with his team, perhaps for a meal together. However, that was for the future – they had quite a long way to go before they could start to discuss their design outcomes with any third party.

CHAPTER 11

Christmas was coming up fast. Alan had written and telephoned his Mum many times, but he could tell that Gilly was worried about him. Two days before Christmas he drove up to Sunderland, with presents for all – for Gilly, Charles his brother and of course for Alison. Alan had been in communication with them all and all answered they would go to Gilly's for Christmas. When he arrived at his Mum's, Gilly was busy in the kitchen, baking and putting the finishing touches to her Christmas dinner. She was thrilled to see Alan, and she wanted to know everything that had happened and obviously she had been very concerned for him and for her grandchildren. Alan was able to reassure her on his behalf but he was also worried about the children.

The following day, Christmas eve, Alan was able to help Gilly and generally make himself useful. Gilly really was a wonderful person and mother. She was seventy years old and was cooking Christmas lunch for 10 people. It included Charles' wife and two children, and Alison and her husband and their two children. Alan really enjoyed getting his hands dirty, cutting logs, making the fires etc.

Christmas Day dawned and everyone turned up – firstly the neighbours, politely asking whose Bentley was parked outside, but generally wishing Gilly a merry Christmas. She was obviously well liked in the neighbourhood. The family arrived at about 11.00 am and Gilly sat next to the tree handing out presents. To Alan it was just like old times and he loved it. After Lunch Alan told them all that had happened to him and his plans for the future. Both Charles and

Alison told of their families' year. The children were all getting near to university time, and it was interesting to find out what they were all doing. Alan vowed to himself that he would go and see his two children as early in the New Year as possible.

On January 2nd 1995 Alan bade farewell to Gilly with hugs and kisses and drove 360 miles back to Eton Stanton. The car was so comfortable and effortless he enjoyed the drive, stopping only for a sandwich and to fill with petrol. Alan arrived home in good spirits. He had bought a dish-washing machine for Molly but he wanted it installed while she was out, so he gave her a lovely necklace which Molly protested was too expensive – but nevertheless she put it on and admired it in the mirror. For Barbara, Molly's daughter, Alan had bought a full compliment of riding lessons. She was thrilled. A few days later and the dishwasher had been installed and at first Molly didn't notice, but when she did she was so surprised she kissed Alan – something she had never done before.

CHAPTER 12

It was coming up to six months since Alan and Doreen had divorced and Alan had tried many times to get in contact with his daughter Suzanne and son Bill. They did not reply to his letters, would not answer his phone calls, and Alan desperately wanted to know how they were getting on. Suzanne was still at university and the last he had heard about Bill was that he was struggling with his GCSEs. He decided to employ a private investigator who would find out how things were going with his children and whether they needed help or anything. He did not want to upset them further, but he really felt a great responsibility to them and loved them very much.

After a few weeks the investigator reported back that Suzanne seemed to be very happy at university and was doing well. She appeared to have plenty of friends and, as far as he could tell, her studies were going as planned. Bill on the other hand was a different kettle of fish. He had to take his GCSEs, but was in with a bad lot of boys and the investigator suspected that they were taking drugs and also involved with small time robberies. Alan asked the investigator to pursue Bill a bit further and get some real facts that he could act upon.

Within a relatively short space of time the investigator came to see Alan and said he would not like to put down on paper what he had discovered. The story was really quite awful. The boy was taking drugs, was involved with this gang who were intimidating shopkeepers and stealing money, and generally things were going downhill. Alan resolved that he had to make a trip back to the north east and confront Doreen to see if they could start a dialogue going in order to help Bill. The investigator also mentioned that Doreen was now engaged to a chap called Jack Daniels, which meant nothing to Bill.

Alan rang Doreen but she would not speak to him. He rang the headmaster of Bill's school who was very pleased to hear from at least one parent. He was concerned about Bill, as he was playing truant most of the time, although he did however turn up for his art lessons which he obviously really enjoyed. The headmaster also said that Bill could quite easily get good GCSE results if he put his back into it, but he really would have to work remarkably hard over the next three months if he was to do any good. He was very concerned. Alan said things between himself and his ex-wife were at a very low state and he wondered whether it would be possible for him to meet his son Bill in the headmaster's study or similar. "Of course," said the headmaster, "I suggest you come on a Wednesday when hopefully Bill will be in school."

Alan left the following day, meaning to drive straight up to Sunderland to meet up with Bill and then if possible to drive on to Sheffield to meet up with Suzanne. He drove up and booked into an hotel in Sunderland. He had a meal and despite everything slept well.

Next morning the headmaster was really quite delighted to meet up with Alan and suggested they should wait until 11.40am, right at the end of the Art class that Bill would be taking. He would ask the teacher to send Bill to the headmaster's study, while Alan waited outside. "Have a chair," the headmaster said to Bill. "I am concerned of course with your truancy and your lack of interest in most of your subjects other than art. How are things at home?"
"Not good," said Bill, "my mother has another man."
"Do you miss your father?" asked the headmaster.
Bill answered, "Yes, we used to have good fun together, but you know he ran off and I haven't seen him for nearly twelve months."
The headmaster then asked, "Would you like to see him again?"

"Oh I don't know," said Bill "I don't think he wants to see me."

"Oh I think he does," said the headmaster.

"Why do you think that?"

"Well, I have spoken to him about you and he is very concerned that you may not get your GCSEs."

"Well, yes, I would like to see him anyway," said Bill.

At which point the headmaster said, "Well, he's here."

The headmaster got up, walked across to the secretary's door. Alan stood there opened his arms and Bill fell into them sobbing. "Where have you been, where have you been? I've missed you. You walked out on us – you walked out on mum, Suzanne and me!"

Alan replied, "Have you not read my letters?"

"No," said Bill, "we haven't had any letters at all."

"In that case," said Alan, "either the Post Office has lost some eight letters that I have written to you and others that I have written to Suzanne and Doreen, your mother, or else somebody must have stolen them."

Bill looked up. "What do you mean?"

Alan said, "I wrote to you every month, tried to ring you on many occasions, and was not allowed to speak to you."

"What's happened then?" asked Bill.

"I went on holiday at the same time that you went on your outward bound course, and I fell seriously ill. I was really very ill indeed for nearly three months and I was not allowed by the doctor to travel at all. By the time I was healthy your mother had started divorce proceedings and these were virtually completed. Anyway that is all in the past. I think we have got to get you sorted out."

"Where are you living now?" asked Bill.

"Oh that's a long story, but I've had a bit of luck and I have started two new businesses. I am having a house built, a beautiful house and all this is in the south of Cornwall."

"Can I come back with you?" asked Bill.

Alan had been trying to work out how best he could help Bill and had come to the conclusion that the best outcome possible was for Bill to come back with him and to attend the local school. He had already made investigations into getting a private tutor to help over the next few months, taking him up to GCSE level. He felt that this was the only way he could get him away from the gang that he was involved with and from the drug scene. Alan asked, "What would your mother say?"

"Oh she couldn't care less – she's got a new boyfriend you know."

"Well," said Alan, "I can certainly get you into the local school and I think get some additional help between now and your GCSEs. You know the important thing, whatever happens, is for you to get good results in your GCSEs."

"I know that," said Bill, "and I have been worried to death."

"OK," said Alan, "let's go and see your mum."

Fortunately Doreen was at home and opened the door to them. "What do you want?" she asked, looking at Alan. Bill explained, "I am going to stay with Dad for a little while and finish my GCSEs."

"That's a good idea," Doreen replied, "when are you going?"

"Now," said Bill, and he pushed past her and ran upstairs to his room.

Doreen said to Alan, "You'd better wait in the car then." So Alan went back to the car and waited. He rang Molly on the phone and told her he was bringing his son Bill back with him and asked if she could try to find some local accommodation. He next rang the school at Eden Stanton. "Can I speak to the headmaster please?" The headmaster came on the line. "This is Alan Brown, regarding the matter that we talked about the other day. I would very much like to take you up on your offer to have Bill in the GCSE classes and also take up the suggestion of a tutor. I think the first thing is that I would like to bring him round, hopefully tomorrow morning."

Alan had been waiting for about half an hour. In fact, he had turned on the radio for some soft music and had fallen asleep. A tap on the window woke him. It was Bill with two large suitcases bursting at the seams with about everything he owned in them, which Alan stuck in the boot. Bill was fascinated with the car – it really was beautiful, with plenty of room, comfortable seats and a powerful engine. "How can you afford a car like this?" asked Bill. "Well, it's a long story," said Alan, "and I will tell you all about it one day. It is a long drive and you have had a long day, I suggest you sit back and close your eyes and let me do some driving." They stopped en-route and had a good meal.

Alan was really quite surprised that Bill did not seem to be taking drugs or anything like that, so he asked him. Bill said, "Oh I don't take them as a rule, just occasionally when I am with the gang. I'm glad to get away from them." "Well son, let me tell you a little about Eden Stanton." Alan proceeded to describe the village, the docks, the fishing boats and some of the people. He told him about Molly, who had taken him in and about her husband who had died well over a year ago now. He described the house he was building with Josh, and about the shipyard he had bought and how he was designing this super fast yacht. Bill was excited by everything and was looking forward to spending time there.

It was quite late in the evening when they reached Eden Stanton. They stopped outside Molly's house and she was at the door waiting for them. They put the cases into the front door and Alan took the car round and parked it up. Molly was already talking to Bill when Alan entered the room. "You've got a good looking son here," she remarked to Alan, "and intelligent too from what I can gather." "Oh yes," said Alan, "I'm sure he's all of that, he's a chip off the old block you know!" They all laughed. Molly told them that she had found accommodation for Bill next door but one, with her cousin Vera. She had lost her husband in the same disaster that took Molly's husband.

They had a cup of tea and a cake and Bill asked, "Did you really nurse my father back to health?" "Yes," said Molly, "it took an awful long time and we were really very worried. The doctor came twice a day at first and gradually your dad pulled round and I'm glad to say that he is still with us. He is a great man you know. He has fitted into village life and is one of our leading stars now."

They walked to Vera's house, where she had the front room ready. "I've never had a lodger before," she said, "but I'm quite looking forward to it. I hope you behave yourself!" When Alan and Bill took the cases up to the room it was exactly like the one that Alan had next door but one. "Ok," said Alan, "I'm going off to bed now. Put your clothes away neatly and I'll pick you up at 10.30 am with your best bib and tucker on, please." "Ok," said Bill, "goodnight father, thank you for coming for me."

Two days later everything was fixed up. The school had accepted Bill and a tutor had been engaged on the specific subjects that he felt needed attention. Bill had promised never to take any drugs whatsoever and Alan felt he could trust him. He was not really involved in the drug scene, thank goodness.

Alan's mind went to Suzanne who by now would have undoubtedly heard the news from Doreen. Just exactly what she had heard Alan knew not. He wrote a short letter to Suzanne saying he was coming to Sheffield University on the following Tuesday and that he would like to meet up with her – could she please confirm a suitable time and meeting place. By the Monday morning following there was no reply.

The detective had told Alan that Suzanne went in the cafeteria nearly every morning, but particularly on a Tuesday at about 11.00am and she usually stayed there for an hour.

Tuesday morning came. He arrived at the university at about 11.15 am and went straight to the cafeteria. He recognised a waitress as someone he had known many years ago, and he asked her help to find a private room where he could wait. The waitress, who knew

Suzanne, agreed to send her into the room when Suzanne arrived at the cafeteria without telling her who was waiting for her.

Alan discretely wandered across to the directors' lounge area, closed the door behind him and sat with a coffee and a newspaper propped up in front of his face. A few minutes later the door opened and in walked Suzanne. "Excuse me," she said, "I believe you wanted to see me?" "Yes," said Alan still hiding behind the newspaper, "come and sit down here." Suzanne did as she was bid.

When Alan lowered the paper she gasped, "What are you doing here?"
Alan replied, "I've come to see you and I think it is very important that we talk for a moment or two."
"I believe you have abducted Bill," she said.
"Look," said Alan, "that is total rubbish and nonsense and you know it is, there is no way that I could or would abduct Bill. Also I believe that the stories you have heard about me are just totally untrue."
"Well," said Suzanne, "we heard that you had run off with another woman and left us."
"That is totally untrue" said Alan, "when your mother went on holiday with her friends, both you and Bill were on your separate holidays and I went off for a week's holiday by myself. When I got there I fell very seriously ill – in fact I was unconscious for two days. It took nearly three months for me to get on my feet and by the time I did your mother was well advanced with divorce proceedings. I had of course written many times to Doreen, your mother, and I had written to both Bill and you, in fact I wrote eight times to you both and not once received a reply."

"I did not know your proper address at university until Bill decided he would come back to my home in Cornwall. That is the absolute truth, Suzanne. I really have come to reassure you that Bill is fine. I thought that he was on drugs and had got into the wrong company and he had, but only to a small extent and I think we can sort that out. But how are you?"

"I'm fine," Suzanne replied, "I am enjoying university and I must admit I didn't really believe all the stories that I heard about you. Mother, as you know, is engaged to be married to this guy who I haven't met yet."

"Look," said Alan, "I will always be here for you, if you would like to come and stay with me in Cornwall I would be delighted. What really matters to you now is to get a good degree. Complete your studies here in Sheffield. If you would like to come down in your break times in the summer let me know. You have my address. In fact I'm learning to fly a light aircraft and hopefully within the next two months I should be able to fly solo and I could come and get you if you like?"

"Oh that would be fun," said Suzanne.

Suzanne glanced at her watch, "Look I'm very sorry, I have a lecture at 12.00. Are you staying for long?"

"No," said Alan, "I think we have cleared the air and we will get together before too long, please Suzanne keep in touch and do reply to my letters."

"Ok," she said and Alan asked for a kiss. She fell into his arms sobbing, "I love you Daddy, I love you."

Alan travelled home with a light heart. Things had worked out well, a lot better than he had expected. He felt that he had got both his children back on line.

CHAPTER 13

Over the next few months Bill was introduced to all Alan's new friends and his business in the shipyard and they went together to look at the house. The house was taking shape – the walls were going up pretty rapidly and the first floor level was soon reached. The aim now was to get the roof on and the windows in so the place could be watertight. Alan had hoped that the house would be ready to move into before Christmas, but Josh advised that it would be March before it was ready and not to rush and spoil it.

He suggested Alan look around for suitable furnishings, which was a totally new thought as Alan had not considered the interior decoration – he needed help. With a bit of a twinkle in his eye, Josh said that he knew a young lady who was extremely good on interior decor. Her name was Julia and Josh said he would invite her down to have a meeting.

A few weeks later Julia came to see both Josh and Alan. She was a young woman, in her mid-twenties, and Alan was most impressed with her approach. She said she would make some initial suggestions, and if Alan liked them, they could move towards a contract and she would be delighted to do the interior decor of the house. This was duly agreed, although as Alan said, it was very early days and the house would not be ready until around about Christmas time to start any real decor or furniture buying. Julia advised this was in fact a very good time, as he could pick up items in the New Year sales.

Very little attention had been paid to the farm that Alan had bought. He had taken away 120 acres for his own use with the house. The rest of it, over 500 acres, he had left to Judd Cort, the manager, and his wife Elle. When he had met them on a couple of previous occasions they had an easy and successful meeting. Judd was delighted then that Alan had bought the farm. Alan went round to see them one Sunday morning after church. They welcomed him with open arms and insisted that he stayed for lunch. Alan gladly accepted, especially as he knew Elle was a good cook, and Judd opened a bottle of wine.

"We need to get down to some business Judd," said Alan. Elle cleared the table and the two men started talking. Alan discovered Judd had not had a pay rise in ten years and things were quite hard on the farm. Alan said he would look into it immediately. They talked about what they should do to the farm next and how it should be developed. Judd had obviously spent a lot of time considering 'his' new farm, which was now over 500 acres. He had planned everything very well, but he needed help. Alan agreed and said the 'help' should be a young qualified farmer, and Judd agreed.

Judd mentioned that there was one area up to about 40 acres that would in his opinion be suitable for vine-growing, with an area facing south, sheltered from the wind, and a chalky sub-soil, which he felt would be ideal. Judd admitted that wine growing was something of a hobby with him. Alan was delighted – what an idea! "Go ahead," he said to Judd, "and plan your vines."

Judd also explained, "I recently let some old stables to a young lady who wanted them for horses, principally for her own use, but also to hire out. I don't think there is much opportunity to hire horses here." They decided to have a walk round and look at the stables. The young lady who met them was called Josie Cheetham, about 20 years old. She proudly took them round the stables – they were old and somewhat decrepit, but the yard was clean and the stables re-whitewashed. There were three horses in excellent condition.

In addition to the stables she had also rented a field from Judd and she asked him whether it was possible to have another field to use for grazing. She was obviously a very keen horsewoman who competed in dressage events. Alan said he didn't think there would be much interest in hiring horses. Josie replied, "Not at the moment, but I think the holidaymakers may well be persuaded – it is a wonderful way to explore and see the countryside. I definitely need to start earning some income. I would like to do it fulltime." Alan wished her the best of luck and added that if he could help her at all he would do. He said goodbye to Judd and Elle, thanked them for the meal and said he would like to set up some sort of meeting with them about every two months if that was alright. They welcomed the idea.

As Alan drove back down to the village he began to think about the young lady with the horses. "I wonder if I could learn to ride," he thought "Maybe have my own horse – it would be great fun. I know that Suzanne did a little bit of riding and was keen to do more, at least this was when she was younger." The more he thought about it the more he decided to do something about it. He rang Josie before he got back to Molly's. "Can you teach me to ride?" he asked.

"I would be delighted to," replied Josie, "When would you like to come?"

"When are you free?" said Alan.

"Any time" said Josie, "but the early morning is the best time."

"What time is early morning?" asked Alan.

"Oh round about seven o'clock."

"What about tomorrow morning?" asked Alan, "there's no time like the present!" "Wonderful" said Josie, "see you then."

Next morning Alan turned up in some old jeans, an open-necked shirt and a sweater. He apologised for being somewhat underdressed. "I must admit," said Josie, "if you want to do this seriously you need to buy some jodhpurs and riding boots." "Well let's see how we get on" said Alan.

Josie chose the quietest horse she had and they went round and round the field, walking at first and then trotting. This was quite difficult. Alan was bouncing all over the place, but at least he didn't fall off. He quickly got the idea, rising to the trot. Josie said, "We've probably done enough for the first lesson." To Alan's surprise nearly two hours had gone by. He had thoroughly enjoyed it and Josie was certainly a good horsewoman and knew how to teach. He booked another lesson for the Thursday at 7.00 am.

Molly wondered what had happened when he suddenly started getting up at 6.30am and was quite surprised when she found out that he was taking riding lessons. "Oh you need to get some riding gear," she said, "why don't you go to Mr Davidson's, he has all types of riding gear, I'm sure he can fix you up." So Alan did. He bought a pair of jodhpurs, riding boots and a jacket and they all fitted and looked perfect. He also bought a weather-proof cape which he hoped would be a useful adjunct. He turned up on the Thursday morning in all his new gear and Josie was delighted. They had another enjoyable two hour session and he booked for the following Monday at 7.00am.

Alan was really enjoying life. He was now well into this horse riding business. Twice a week he was also learning to fly. Again he was doing two two-hour sessions of flying each week, so he was coming on very fast. In another three weeks he hoped he would be able to do his first solo flight.

CHAPTER 14

Alan's business was developing on all fronts and really moving very quickly. It was now March 1993, when he was invited to the Cornwall Law Society's Dinner by James Lord. At the dinner he sat next to a young accountant, Jeremy Knight, and they talked together as much as were able at a dinner, but Alan made a mental note to contact Jeremy again in future. He decided to do this sooner rather than later so he rang and made an appointment. Jeremy had been an accountant with a large firm of accountants in London for six years. However, he had been brought up in the country and felt that his vocation was to be an accountant to the farming community and that Cornwall was a very good place to start his own practice.

When Alan visited Jeremy he first of all asked him if he would sign a paper of non-disclosure, saying that he recognised that once they were working together this would not be necessary. However, Alan felt that he wanted to explain all of his business to Jeremy and allow him to make a decision as to whether he was the right accountant to cover these fields. Jeremy gladly agreed to sign the document and they sat down to discuss.

Alan explained about the Cornwall shipyard, its current activities in converting fishing boats to pleasure craft and his ideas of developing a very fast cruiser yacht which were now becoming well advanced. He also explained about the development that was taking place on the EHS. Alan told Jeremy that he had bought Home Farm with about 600 acres, and that he would like to turn the farm over to organic farming with the hope of developing this concept across the whole of Cornwall if possible. He recognised one of the problems was selling the produce at a higher price, although he felt that he may be able to overcome this by opening his own supermarket chain.

Some of Alan's excitement towards the businesses spread to Jeremy. He asked a series of questions and then said, "I would be absolutely delighted to take on your accounts. I would need to take additional staff, but first I would like to look at the business in greater depth." It was of course a huge opportunity for Jeremy, provided everything went according to plan. Alan suggested to Jeremy that it might be necessary to put in new accounting systems. He had not paid much attention to this and was well aware of the necessity to have good systems with a management reporting structure, but the businesses had grown very fast in such a short time. Jeremy said he would look into it quickly, and with that they had a good lunch and Alan headed for home.

A few weeks later Alan made his first solo flight in a light aircraft. It was a two-seater Cessna and he spent about three-quarters-of-an-hour in the air, making three landings, just to show that it was not a 'fluke' the first time. He landed the plane beautifully on each occasion. His instructor was delighted and Alan would receive his wings before too long.

He took the senior instructor across to his new house build, which was to be called *Parklands*. He showed him the driveway and how it ran right past the house, as well as where he intended to put two hangars and a helicopter pad. The instructor was most impressed and felt he would have no difficulty whatsoever in converting his driveway to a landing strip. He gave him a few tips on what was required, but Josh had already started to look into this.

Suzanne rang and asked if she could come for a couple of weeks over the Easter break – she wanted to bring her friend Catherine who was an orphan and had nowhere to go in the holidays. She felt very sorry for her and they got on very well together. Alan said they could come with the greatest of pleasure. Alan felt that with Bill, Suzanne, Catherine and himself, it would be a good opportunity to rent a small house which they could run between them in the village. He was able to do this and decided he would take it for a whole year until his own house at *Parklands* was fully completed. He would still stay with Molly when he was by himself and Bill would stay with Vera where he was very happy, but he could see that Suzanne and possibly other friends would come again for an extended period in the summer.

He rang Suzanne back and said that he would fly up to Sheffield to a landing strip and bring the two of them back down to Cornwall. It meant that Alan could get his flying hours in, which was important, but he decided that as he was going quite a long distance for his maiden flight he would ask one of the instructors to come with him.

They flew up early in April in a seven-seater twin-engine plane. They set out early in the morning but it was only just over three hours flight to Sheffield. Alan did all the flying and all the navigating, with the instructor just sat observing – it was nice to have someone he could call on in case of emergency. His instrument flying was still some way off, but on this flight the weather was perfect and he could see the ground all the way. Suzanne and Catherine were waiting at the air strip. They were introduced and climbed aboard very excited and with a fairly fast turnaround they set off back. Again it was an uneventful flight and they landed back at Land's End Aero Club. All four of them had a light lunch at the Aero Club and Alan thanked his instructor for travelling with him.

Driving back home in the Bentley, Suzanne and Catherine were most impressed. It really was a lovely car and it purred along, although the Cornish roads were somewhat narrow for such a large car. Alan asked, "What do you want to do while you are here? Can I make some suggestions?"
"Oh yes please," the girls echoed.

"Well," he said, "every morning we could go riding. Do you like riding?"

Again they both echoed, "Yes." Although Catherine had done very little, she still enjoyed it. Suzanne had ridden quite a lot as a young girl in her early teens and was quite an accomplished horsewoman.

"Also," he said, "it's time you learnt to drive. Would you like to have some driving lessons?"

"Oh yes, certainly we would," Suzanne said, "but we've only got a fortnight."

Alan replied, "Well you could come back again in the summer; it would give you an introduction anyway."

Both girls were absolutely delighted and Alan promised to take them to see the farm and the shipyard, but he didn't at this stage mention the other development. Bill was delighted that he could show them the way with the horses, but was a little jealous that they were learning to drive and he wasn't old enough as yet. Alan explained that he was building a new house, but that it would not be ready for almost a year, so in the meantime he had rented this small house which he hoped they would be happy in. The house was in the centre of the village, close to the harbour, and there was as much activity going on as there possibly could be in such a small village. The fishing boats of course went out every day and came back first thing in the morning. The fish market was an interesting place to visit – it was a hive of activity for several hours each morning.

Alan took them up to *Parklands* to see the house being built and showed them the plans, and again they were most impressed and thought it would be absolutely super. He introduced them to Josh who was always on the site for at least some part of every day. He explained about the driveway and how he hoped to convert it into a light aircraft runway, and they walked around where he hoped to put the herds of deer. Suzanne was really excited at the prospect of deer being on the park and she was also really interested in Judd's farm. Judd agreed to take her for a couple of days to show her the ropes and Suzanne really enjoyed this.

63

They managed to get the riding in every morning, riding to different parts of the countryside round about. Catherine had been given a rather timid and easy horse to ride and very quickly she wanted something with a little bit more spirit. Nevertheless she thoroughly enjoyed the riding and both girls also developed well with their driving, having two lessons a week. They stayed an extra week, before Alan, again with the instructor, flew them back to Sheffield. The airport they used was the Robin Hood airport – although 18 miles from Sheffield it was the only airport available to them.

Both Catherine and Suzanne wrote to Alan to thank him for their wonderful three weeks at Eden Stanton, and Suzanne explained that Catherine had remarked on what a super guy he was, and how lucky she was to have a father like that. Suzanne also said that they were both looking forward to coming back in the summer for a long period of time, if that were possible.

Alan was delighted that both his children were really back on line and back in his life. Bill was working very hard for his exams and was conscious that he had to make up the bit of time he had lost. His tutor and headmaster felt that he would do well. Suzanne he knew was a natural at university, and he was hoping that she might get a 'first', but that remained to be seen.

A couple of weeks went by and Jeremy Knight, the accountant, rang Alan and asked to come and see him. They met up at the shipyard in Alan's office. Jeremy said there were a number of technical things that needed to be set up. "Your year end, whilst not due at the moment, needs to be settled and a proper management accounting structure put in place. This goes for all the businesses, as the scanner development is quite an expensive process, and you need to be aware of the costs as they are occurring." He confirmed to Alan that the shipyard was doing well and highly profitable, although again quit a lot of money was being spent on development of the yacht, and he also foresaw that there would be considerably high costs in tooling required for the yacht.

The farm was progressing well – it wasn't highly profitable, but it was run efficiently and he felt he could take a little step back, but he still wanted to put a new system in. He also suggested to Alan that it may be advantageous for him to employ his own in-house accountant, not necessarily a fully qualified accountant. He had a mind a man of about 35 years old who was well experienced, not qualified, but really as good as any accountant. If he oversaw the new systems being put in, Jeremy felt that this guy could be a big asset, particularly in view of the development that Alan had outlined to him. Alan agreed and said he would like to meet up with this person that Jeremy had recommended.

They met up two weeks later. His name was Andrew McBride, a Scotsman. Alan had always gone along with the joke that the Scots were a mean lot and if you wanted a good accountant then choose a Scotsman! They got on together immediately. Although Andrew was a bit dower, but seemed very sound and was very keen indeed to move to Cornwall. His wife had been brought up in the country, whereas he was a Glaswegian. Alan offered him the job almost immediately and he accepted it. He would start on 1st July.

At the beginning of March that year Gerald, the boat designer, felt he was sufficiently advanced with his whole design and asked permission for a scale model to be made and to be tested in a marine test tank. The model had now been made and was ready to test. Everyone connected with the project drove up to the Wolfson Unit at Southampton Solent University where the test facility had been hired for the whole day. Firstly the equipment was tested for stability just anchored, and then moving at a low speed of about five knots through the water, moving on to storm conditions. It stood up to all of this, did not capsize and performed very well.

The next test propelled it up to about 15 knots to start bringing the pontoons into action, when the boat lifted out of the water and was able to accelerate rapidly. It worked perfectly and as the boat lifted the engines were automatically lowered. Various sea conditions were tested and the boat performed brilliantly up to 80 knots.

However, at about 80 knots, the boat started to vibrate violently and they had to bring the speed down quite quickly. At 70-75 knots it was totally stable, with no vibrations at all, so it was felt that at 65 knots (which was Alan's original guestimate) the craft would be absolutely perfect. Gerald was really quite amazed that there were no major alterations required – in fact there were very little amendments to make at all. It was extremely detailed testing. The test engineers operating the whole project congratulated him on a first-class model – although it was of course only the model.

On the way home talk was all about getting the first prototype into the water. Alan decided to go straight for a fibreglass hull. This meant a major expense with the moulds. One of the rather novel ideas that both he and Gerald had come up with was that there was to be quite a large gap between the inner and outer hulls. This allowed for liquid storage – water, fuel, etc, but it also was a major buoyancy area in a series of tanks right round the vessel. The engines were in pods, which had proved themselves and were hung at the sides of the stern of the boat and lowered into the water, saving considerable space within the side of the boat itself. The overall length of the boat had been fixed at 20m with a 7.5m beam.

Gerald reckoned that he needed a further month now for the plans to be completed to allow it to go forward for the moulds for the fibreglass – it was extremely detailed work. They had previously gone out to three companies and decided upon one specific manufacturer, whom they now contacted. The owner of the company was absolutely delighted to get the work to do such a prestigious project. It was a large fibreglass moulding, so it would be toward the end of August before they could be delivered. This fitted in very well with the construction of the new shed and also allowed Gerald to get on with the sail design, deck fitting design, etc. Also one of his 'boys', as he called them, was extremely good at interior boat design and so he would put him on to this straight way.

Everything on the boat side was progressing very well. The designs that Gerald put in for the conversion of the fishing boats were working extremely well and the customers were delighted with the outcome. They were now actually on the water and taking visitors out to see the various sights around the coast. The order book in the yard was going up, such that they could not complete enough conversions. They had also, unbelievably, received an order for a new fishing boat. Gerald wanted to spend a bit of time on looking at the design of this, rather than just do a standard design as previously done. He was a busy man, as was the whole of the dockyard staff.

CHAPTER 15

Bill, despite all the interruptions from being so interested in everything that his father was doing, stuck to his studies and had started his GCSEs with great optimism. By the end of June he had sat all his exams and felt that he would have pretty good results – it was now a matter of waiting. He spent time furiously thinking about what he would do with the rest of his life and which university he would go to, and what subjects he would take. Bill had a real yarn for architecture. He loved the idea of designing things, particularly buildings. He had researched various universities and although Sheffield was an option, Cardiff was the top university, with Bath close behind. Alan and he discussed all of this at length and finally decided on Cardiff first, with Bath a good second.

Suzanne wrote to say that she had also completed her three exams and was waiting for results, as had her friend Catherine. They would both like very much to spend the entire summer holidays with Alan and both think about what they were going to do with their lives. Alan was of course delighted and began to think a little of what they could do. They had of course the horse riding, and hopefully the completion of their learning to drive. In addition Alan thought it would be rather nice to hire a yacht, say of between 40ft and 60ft, maybe for the whole of July and August, and sail up the coast. Above all that ,they each had to think, Bill included, about their future. It was a serious time in their lives for all of them.

Alan realised that he hadn't been to see his mother since the previous Christmas and it was now towards the end of June. He had kept in touch with her by correspondence and the odd telephone call, so he knew that she was very well and hearty, but Alan had always gone round to his mum's house and kept in weekly contact with her ever since his father and brother had been killed. He also realised that in three weeks time it was her 80th birthday. He had written the odd letter to his brother, Charles, and sister, Alison, and both had responded. So he wrote to them both and suggested they should do something about their mother's 80th birthday. Both of them had remained around the north east and were not too far way. Charles was a mechanical engineer and was doing quite well, married with two children. Alison was married, a veterinary surgeon and also had two children. The three of them had not seen each other since Christmas and Alan was really looking forward to a family reunion.

Alison was the first to call him and she suggested that they all went out and had a lunchtime meal – she had in mind a local restaurant and had already rung them, and they had a private room which would accommodate up to 40 people. Alison went through a list of aunts and uncles who were still living and she reckoned that with their own children they would possibly get up to about 25 people. Alan thought she had done brilliantly and asked her if she would book the restaurant. Charles would have to fit in, so the date was set for 23rd July. Alan immediately booked a local hotel for Suzanne, Catherine, Bill and himself for the night of 22nd, and rang Charles to tell him what had been organised and hoped that he agreed with this. Charles of course agreed and said he was looking forward to meeting up with Alan and his family. He suggested that two near-neighbours who had been keeping their eye on mother should also be invited. Alan readily agreed and asked Charles if he would speak to Alison and organise it between them.

He flew up to Sheffield the following day, taking Bill with him and this time flying without the instructor. They had a good flight, picked up Suzanne and Catherine and came back home. It was quite uneventful and this was becoming a regular trip. Alan thoroughly enjoyed flying. They all had a lovely meal that night at a local restaurant and then retired early to the house that Alan had rented for the summer. He talked to them about his ideas for the holidays and they thought that renting a yacht would be absolutely splendid. Suzanne was a little concerned about where her future lay and wanted to get that settled as soon as possible.

Alan also told them about the arrangements for their grandma's 80th birthday, and they all decided that they would like to spend a little time in a nearby town to see if they could find a suitable present for Grandma.

The next morning they all went riding at 7.00 pm, as Alan did every day. They were looking forward to doing this nearly every day of the holiday. Suzanne also organised their driving lessons as she wished to pass her test as soon as possible. They got a young lad from the shipyard to drive them a few miles up the coast to pick up the yacht. It was splendid – a 50ft yacht, about 10 years old, but it sailed beautifully and they had a lovely trip back to Eden Stanton. They moored up in the harbour and looked forward to some serious sailing, possibly across to France. It was going to be a busy summer holiday.

Gilly's birthday quickly came and Alan flew them all up to Sunderland. The nearest air landing strip was at Durham Tee Valley Airport, so Alan had arranged a car to be available there. Gilly was delighted to see them all. She was really very well, quite active and with a good brain on her. She was the mother that Alan always remembered. Alan explained, "We are going to take you out tomorrow and have some lunch together, if that is alright?" Gilly said, "Oh that would be fine." So Alan told her, "Put your best bib and tucker on – it's a nice restaurant that we are going to go to."

Gilly was delighted to see the grandchildren. She had not seen either of them for over ten months and they told her everything that they had been doing. As soon as the house was completed, Alan said that he would like Gilly to come down and spend some time with them, but this would not be until after Easter next year. However, he said that they would all come up for Christmas and have Christmas Day with her.

Gilly was thrilled that the family were back together. She had really wondered what on earth had happened and was very worried for them. Her life was quite comfortable – the money situation was fine, she had a nice bungalow, the one that Alan had bought for her when the compensation money came through, and she got on well with the neighbours who popped in from time to time.

The next day Alan and the children picked Gilly up and took her to the restaurant. They went through to the private room where, to her surprise, all the rest of her family and friends had gathered to wish her a happy birthday. They had a super meal and a huge birthday cake with 80 candles, which Gilly had great difficulty blowing out! Afterwards all the presents that they had bought her were opened. Gilly had spent most of the time in joyful tears, and she had had a wonderful day. When Alan took her back home she was tired out. Alan spent the evening with his sister Alison and her family, and he suggested that they all got together again at Christmas.

They arrived back at Eden Stanton the following day, and both Suzanne and Catherine wrote a multitude of letters to prospective employers. They both decided that they loved Cornwall and out of preference would really like to stay in that part of the world.

Bill got his results. He had done really well with his exams and he was able to confirm that he would be going to Bath University. Alan also knew that within one of his companies he could employ Suzanne, a manufacturing engineer, who was undoubtedly good on the organisation side. Catherine had specialised in servo mechanics at university and he felt that the shipyard would certainly benefit from her knowledge, but he mentioned neither of these things, preferring that they would gain experience elsewhere and stand on their own feet – even if this meant them moving away.

Alan asked Gerald Birch if he would like to accompany them on sailing the yacht across to France for a few days, and if it were possible for his fiancée Jane, who was a doctor, to come with them. Gerald was a good sailor and Alan felt they needed his expertise. Also he thought it was an ideal opportunity for him to meet Suzanne and Catherine and see whether some time in the future, perhaps they could join the company.

They intended to take five or six days sailing across to France. Catherine had never been out of England before so they rushed to get a passport in case they needed it.

The appointed day arrived so Alan, Bill, Suzanne, Catherine, Gerald and Jane boarded the yacht. It was some time since Alan had met Jane who was a delightful young lady born in the north of England, Lancashire, but had found her way down to Cornwall, part of the country which she really did love. She had met Gerald at university purely by accident, being in the wrong place as it happened at the right time. They were obviously very much in love and it was really delightful to see. It brought back memories to Alan of his university days with Susan. What a mess he had made of that, but he had two lovely children and he had the opportunity to live out a dream.

They sailed steadily for about twelve hours reaching the French coast, cruising around into Cherbourg. It had been a super trip. Catherine in particular had thoroughly enjoyed it. No one had been sea sick. It was Jane's first sea trip as well, although she was a good dingy sailor. Since they had had such a good trip over Alan thought it might be a nice idea to go round the corner down to Alderney and then sail back from the Channel Isles. They arrived back home five days later and had had a wonderful week which had introduced them all to sea sailing.

Alan hoped that this was would be the beginning of family excursions when his new boat arrived in under a year's time now. In fact Gerald said that the fibreglass moulds were due to arrive the next week. Alan was determined to be there when they arrived.

The moulds arrived on time. A special carrying jig had been made, as the whole of one piece was huge – 20m in length, 7.5m in width. They decided having got it on the floor, if they fitted suitable wheels to the jig, they would be able to move it around the workshop as required. There were a lot of different moulds – there was the hull, the inside of the boat which was almost as big as the hull (and when the two fitted together this would give various watertight compartments throughout the sides and underneath of the vessel), the cabin roof and the moulds for the pontoons which came out of the side of the vessel. Gerald and his team examined every inch of the moulds looking for any slight defect or problem, but there were none. They really were first-class.

The next stage was to fit all the electric and plumbing into the cavities between the two skins before they were put together. This was meticulous work. The wiring loom itself was a major job. Gerald had made this in advance so that it was ready for just placing in the boat, but it took several days. Alan was delighted that his yacht was taking shape and couldn't wait to get it on the water and test its performance. It would be another three months before it was ready. That would possibly take them to the bad weather of the wintertime. Everyone was impatient. Jim Caldwell, the production manager, was tearing his hair out as he had so much work on, and Gerald was pinching the best of his crew to play with this silly yacht, or so he thought.

Both Suzanne and Catherine found a job within the same company, quite independently. They had written to an international design engineering company which had offices throughout the world, and both of them felt that it would give them a much broader experience. They were to start the first week in September.

One morning Alan was in his office at the boat yard and John Stevens and Alistair Roberts, the two guys in charge of the EHS burst into his office, jumping up and down with excitement. "What's the matter?" asked Alan.

"Nothing's the matter," replied Alistair, "we have just had a major breakthrough, can we tell you about it?"

"Of course" said Alan.

"Well, by playing with the electronics, with the accuracy with which John could do the mechanics he was able to penetrate the hull of a steel ship 20 miles off shore. We are able to pick out certain items and tell whether there are drugs on board – well, particular types of drug, heroine, cannabis and so on and also we can tell whether there are people stowed aboard."

"That's fantastic!" said Alan, "is there any limitation?"

"Oh, there is one serious one," said Alistair, "we cannot get below sea level, so provided all the gear or the people are stowed above sea level we can see them quite clearly."

"I think this is a major breakthrough though," remarked Alan, "we can use this for all sorts of purposes, not just sea bound. Look, you two you have been working almost solidly now for nine months and I don't think either of you have taken a break. Why don't you go off and do so. Lock the place up until you come back."

Alistair added, "This is so exciting – it's really a fantastic breakthrough."

"I know that," said Alan "just take a week's holiday, stay at a good hotel, get away from each other, see your families, have a break."

John agreed. "I'd like to visit my parents and see my sister. I haven't seen her for a year."

"Right," said Alan, "I think that's settled. I know you are excited, I know it's a major breakthrough, and I am just as enthusiastic as you are, but it would do you both good to have a break." Finally Alistair also agreed.

Alan said, "When you get back come and see me and we'll have a good brainstorming session about where we are going."

Ten days later they sat together again round the office table and had a really good brainstorming session. This black box they had developed could be used on land to examine trucks. "Now what do we do?" asked Alan. "Do we progress the original concept of looking at ships passing within 20 miles of the coast, or do we change tack?"

Alistair said, "I think we could really do both, because the original concept is very nearly completed. We have to tidy it up, but it works. We are able to continually scan the horizon with two binocular type viewers. We can pick up any change in speed or major direction of any of the vessels. We are able to spot any small craft going out from the shore and meeting up with those vessels, and can examine whether there is any transfer of people or goods even – we can see it quite clearly. All of this information is passed through a computer and the computer does all the work continuously, 24-hours a day reporting anything untoward. It works, it really does work, and I think that it is robust enough to go on working for many years. We would be able to couple the computer up to a data link and so pass the information to the authorities whoever that might be."

"OK," said Alan, "that sounds pretty conclusive, are you able to give a good demonstration?"

"Oh definitely," said Alistair and John agreed.

"I don't want to broadcast this, so I am going to have to be very careful how I go about selling it," said Alan. "I am going to aim for the Prime Minister and possibly the Defence Minister, but certainly no one below."

Alistair added, "This is something that will go down well in the States."

"Yes", said Alan, "let me see how I go on with the PM and then I'll tackle America. Do you feel able to develop this system that we talked about for trucks, vans and cars?"

"Definitely," replied Alistair.

"Is it possible it could be put on a hand-carrying device?"

"I think so," answered Alistair, "I was thinking along the same lines."

"OK, you two, extremely well done. I am delighted. Let's see if we can make some money out of this now and please make sure that you take your breaks and holidays – it is so important, as you have just recognised."

They both agreed and off they went.

The following week Alan went down to the lighthouse and had a full demonstration. It was extremely impressive. The computer talked them through exactly what was happening and they were able to pull up one particular evening when they spotted a small boat going out and meeting up with a large tanker. The three men in the small boat reached the tanker and one got off and headed up the outside ladder. He was handed a parcel by someone, they presumed the captain, came down the ladder back into the boat and then returned to land. They could tell that the parcel contained heroine, a large quantity.

"Have we reported this?" asked Alan.

"No", said John.

"We really need to settle where we are going with this," said Alan.

He wrote to the Prime Minister, marked 'For your eyes only', and briefed him on the concept of what they were trying to achieve. He pointed out that they had now fully achieved their aims but did not want this information to be on general release. He could demonstrate this but it would have to be a very close number of people. Two weeks later he had heard nothing. He wrote again and asked for a personal interview with the PM. Again he heard nothing. Not even an acknowledgement of his letter. Alan was fuming and really thought it was ignorant.

CHAPTER 16

During his investigations into which light plane he should buy he had come across a mechanic who worked at the weekend at the small field aerodrome where he had learnt to fly. The man was an American called Chuck. He was principally employed by the United States Air Force base, just five miles up the road. His passion was light aircraft and he was a whizz with them. Alan asked about the Commanding Officer at the base. Chuck told him that it was an Ian McKenzie, a very approachable guy who did not stand much on ceremony. Alan put the information to the back of his mind. A couple of weeks later, when he still hadn't had any reply from the Prime Minister regarding the EHS, he pulled this information from the back of his mind, took the bull by the horns and rang up Ian McKenzie.

He actually got through to the Commander in person. Alan explained, "I'm building a house just down the road from the base, probably about five miles, but it won't be ready until next April."
"We wondered whose the construction was," said Ian, "we have noticed it as we have flown overhead, it looks like an impressive place."
"Well, it's not as big as perhaps it looks from the air," replied Alan. "I would welcome the opportunity to meet up with you. Could I come and see you?"
"Of course you can, any time, why not come and have lunch with me today?"
"That's fine by me," said Alan, "thank you very much".

So Alan drove up to the base. They got on famously. Ian was an easy-going guy who knew his job. Alan said, "I have an ulterior motive in meeting up with you."

"Oh, I thought you would," said Ian. Alan told him briefly about the concept of the scanner. "That sounds a fantastic machine."

"Well," said Alan, "I'd like to demonstrate it to you in order that I could use your name writing to the President."

"Wow," said Ian. "I have an idea – the Commander of all American Forces in Europe, based in Germany, is coming across here to spend a few days with me. I think he could be very interested and his name would go a lot further than mine with the President. I'll invite you for lunch again and then you can meet him."

"Oh," said Alan, "that is very generous of you and a great idea, but I can't keep using your hospitality like this. I find it quite difficult to respond with no house to live in at the moment."

"That's OK," said Ian, "I can't wait to come and visit you when you get into the house. That would be a splendid thing." At that moment his wife Veronica walked in. "Ah," said Ian, "Veronica, meet Alan Brown, one of our local entrepreneurs. I am going to invite him across to meet Bob Calendar next week."

"That's a great idea," said Veronica, "his wife would be with him, why don't we make an evening of it, perhaps you could bring your wife over?"

Alan replied, "Unfortunately I am divorced, but I have an extremely attractive daughter who I am sure would love to come and visit you."

"Right then, that's fixed" said Ian.

A week later, on the Saturday night, Alan and Suzanne made their way to the American Air Base. Ian introduced them to Bob Calendar and his wife Jasmine. They were extremely nice people and very welcoming. They had an exceptionally good meal of the highest standard and Suzanne was soon at ease. She made a great impression and Alan was very proud. When they had finished the meal Veronica took the ladies, Jasmine and Suzanne out into the lounge, leaving the men with their port.

"Right," said Ian, "I have updated Bob, albeit very briefly I must confess, on what we talked about – perhaps you would like to expand a little?"

Alan said, "Firstly I want to thank you both for giving me this opportunity and for your wonderful hospitality. Secondly I must say that I would like this conversation to go no further than the three of us. I believe that it could become very sensitive information. Can I have your assurance on that?" They both agreed. Alan continued, "What I wish to do is to inform the American Government, and I think at Presidential level, about this project. I need to have some credibility and I am hoping that both of you would give me that. I would like to take the opportunity to lay on a demonstration in the next day or so, while you are here Bob, to see what you think."

Bob said, "If it'll do what you say it will do, then it really is a major breakthrough. This could be very sensitive, and I would be delighted to witness your demonstration."

They agreed that this could take place on Monday morning and Alan would come to the base and pick them up. They finished their port and joined the ladies.

On the way home Suzanne was bubbling. "What really nice people," she said, "I've not met any Americans before." Alan replied, "You must realise dear that you are dealing with some of the top people in America there, and I agree with you that it was a lovely evening and they are very nice people."

CHAPTER 17

Alan warned John and Alistair to expect VIP visitors on Monday morning. They said they were all ready. On Monday morning Alan drove up with his Bentley to the Air Force Base and Bob and Ian were waiting. "For security reasons my man has to come with us, I hope that is OK?" "No problem" said Alan and they set off. They arrived at the lighthouse and went inside. The security guard remained outside the demonstration room, and John and Alistair were introduced. Alistair explained that whilst this was a prototype machine, and perhaps looked a little 'Heath Robinson', it worked extremely efficiently and had been doing so for some time.

They had tidied the systems up and effectively produced a black box, a rather large one, but nevertheless they were not seeing the completely finished article, but one that certainly did the job. It was an impressive demonstration. Any ship that deviated speed or direction was reported, any vessel that left the land was reported. It showed the small craft approaching the large tanker and the man boarding, goods being handed over and the small vessel coming back to land.

"Now," said Alistair, "I would like to turn it on to live so you can see and hear exactly what is happening at this moment." It was very fortunate that there were several large tankers going up the channel, as well as several smaller ships at the time. The computer picked out one vessel in particular which slowed right down, almost to a stop. "It's unfortunate," remarked Alistair, "that we cannot see whether there is anything approaching from the other side of the vessel, we can only view it from this side." Just at that moment a high speed power boat came into view. It rendezvoused with the vessel that had stopped. Three men went on board. Two of them returned to the power boat and it sped away. One man had been left on the ship.

"This is fantastic," said Bob, "this is really quite unbelievable! To get this detail, and get it automatically reported like this really is quite fantastic. I have never come across anything like it. Just one thing though," he continued, "how did you know that on the demonstration it was heroine that was being transferred?"
Alan stepped in, "We are pretty certain that it was heroine, we are working on a system that can identify drugs, at the moment this is really not for publication."
"Gee that would be quite something," admitted Bob.

Alan took the Americans back to his office in the shipyard. He showed them the prototype yacht which was beginning to really take shape. Bob remarked, "That is an impressive vessel. I'd like one of those." Alan explained that it was capable of 65 knots, that this was the prototype, and as soon as it was up and running he would be very welcome to have a day out on it. "I'd like that very much," said Bob and Ian agreed. They had a cup of coffee in Alan's office and he asked them whether they would be prepared to let him use their names when writing to the President. "Sure," said Bob, "I have no hesitation whatsoever. This is something that really will have to be investigated at the highest level." Alan then drove all three back to the base. Bob was obviously very excited. Alan again said, "Please sir, I hope you will keep it to yourself." "Oh yes, yes," Bob replied.

CHAPTER 18

The yacht was ready for launching. Alan decided to name it *Endeavour* and the whole shipyard turned out to watch the launch. Alan invited Molly to launch it, and she was delighted. A few of them went aboard and they motored it around to the harbour. Alan hoped that within the next few days they would be able to go on a worthwhile trip to test its sailing capabilities and the engines.

Gerald had worked out a whole test programme. It was an exciting time and the weather remained pretty good for the time of the year so that the vessel was conclusively tested over the next four or five weeks. It performed brilliantly – 65 plus knots under sail, the same under power, and all the controls were electronic and bespoke to the boat. It navigated, was aware of what was happening around it through the radar system, and the sails could be adjusted and the engines started and stopped just by voice command.

The cabins below were luxurious – there were three individual cabins with en suite facilities and a further cabin for four people in bunks, again with facilities. The galley was superb and the dining arrangements really beautifully set out. It was a splendid boat – everything that Alan had expected and Gerald had done a wonderful job on it. Alan congratulated all his team. It was now up to Alan to find a method of selling the boat. He decided to enter it for the 'Round Britain Race' the following year.

In the meantime, Alan received a reply from the President of the United States. It came within two weeks of him writing. The

President had contacted both Bob Calendar and Ian McKenzie, and both spoke very highly of the system and advised that it should be further investigated at the highest level. He had asked the Secretary of State to be in contact with a view to having a presentation and trusted that this was a satisfactory arrangement at this stage. Included with the letter was a signed statement from the President of the United States saying that he would not disclose, nor would any of his staff, any information whatsoever regarding this concept, without first seeking permission from Alan. Alan responded immediately, thanked the President and said he was delighted that the Secretary of State was to attend a demonstration.

It was everything that Alan wanted. The Americans were treating it seriously and he really felt he had a huge opportunity to sell the equipment to them. He held a meeting with Alistair and John to decide whether they should try and sell a completed unit manufactured in the UK, or sell them the manufacturing rights and take a royalty with perhaps the opportunity of doing the selling in Europe. Their discussions went on for several hours and unfortunately they didn't reach a conclusion. However, they had aired the pros and cons of various solutions. They decided in the end to give themselves more time for further consideration and thought.

Alan received a phone call from his sister Alison. They discussed what to do about Christmas. Alison had been in touch with Gilly and she wanted Christmas at her house. Alison was worried it would be too much for her with all the children. "Why don't we get outside caterers in, and let's stay in local hotels. Perhaps you, your husband and children could stay with Gilly. We could all meet together on Christmas Day – I think she could cope with that," suggested Alan. Alison thought this was a good plan and agreed to contact Charles and get a caterer whom she knew to do the meal. It would be expensive, because it was Christmas time, but Alan offered to cover it.

Bill broke up for Christmas and still continued to study, he had been bitten by the academic bug. Suzanne and Catherine turned up together a couple of days before Christmas and they all travelled up to Sunderland, this time in the car. Gilly was on great form over Christmas – she really was remarkable for her age and everybody had a superb time. The idea of hiring a caterer in was a good one. Two days later Alan and his crew motored back to Eden Stanton. They had had a lovely Christmas.

Suzanne was really enjoying her work and so was Catherine. They had settled into the new company and were allowed a considerable amount of freedom to do their work. They rented a flat together and Suzanne was saving up to buy a car. Alan said he would help with this, so together they went out and bought a small car. Suzanne was of course delighted – it was her first car and she was 23 years of age now.

CHAPTER 19

In the middle of January Alan received a phone call from the US Secretary of State. She asked if it would be convenient for her to visit the following week and to bring the Secretary of Defence with her. Alan said it would be no problem and asked where she was staying and if he could help.

"Oh no," Condoleezza Rice said, "it's a non-official visit this. Please keep it to yourself – we will be staying at the air base, which I understand is just a mile or two from you?"

"That's right," replied Alan.

"OK look forward to seeing you then."

The following week he got a further phone call to arrange the details and at ten o'clock that morning he met them by the new gates to his house at *Parklands*. There was something of an entourage – two cars, the Secretary of State, the Secretary of Defence, two detectives and a further car with four armed police in it. Alan explained that this was his new house which was almost completed and would be ready in a few months. They followed up the road and parked as near as they could get to the lighthouse.

He had already advised John and Alistair that they would be coming and they were there at the door to welcome them. It was only the Secretary of State and Secretary of Defence who came to the presentation area, all the entourage kept outside. Alistair went through a new presentation. It showed all the facilities of the system. They were totally amazed with the presentation and thought it was unbelievable. Condoleezza Rice asked how robust the system was, and Alistair assured her that it was hardy and endurable. The model they showed them was the latest black box and it looked very compact and business-like.

The Secretary of Defence commented, "We could do with a new fast boat to catch up with the buggers couldn't we now?"
Alan smiled to himself, "We can fulfil that dream as well Mr Secretary."
"How do you mean?" he asked.
"If we've finished here I can show you."

They went to the dock down below the lighthouse where the yacht was moored. "I didn't mean a yacht," he said.
"I know that," replied Alan, "but if you can spare an hour to come on board I think it may be worth your while".
So with a little hesitation the whole entourage boarded. Alan let go the moorings and said, "Head for France, sails only." The boat headed off, the sails unfurled, tautening up as though there were invisible men operating it. "How did you do that?" asked one of the secretaries. "It's all electronic, controlled by word of mouth. I can furl the sail, alter the speed, we can go onto engine, and meanwhile it's giving a watchful brief of everything that is around us so we won't run into anything. How about this – top speed please." The boat more or less took off – 30, 35, 40, 45, 50, 55, 60, 65 knots. It was a very comfortable ride, despite the heavy swell and a few breakers. Alan estimated that there might be a scale four to five blowing at the time.

"Good God man," exclaimed the Secretary of State "What is it?"
"Well," said Alan "it is the prototype of a very upmarket fast cruiser that we are building at my shipyard. I think we could use the same hull moulding with a new deck moulding to build a very fast interceptor vessel that would carry up to 30 marines if necessary. It would be a stealth boat, undetectable by current radar, and practically unseen at night."

"Well," said the Secretary of Defence, "if you could show me one of those, I'd order 200 straight off as a test run."

Alan suggested they came back to his office but Condoleezza said, "No, I'd rather that we just kept it in-house. If you don't mind please come back with us to the US Base and we can discuss some details." After some discussion on the EHS Alan asked, "Have you any idea or concept as to how many are likely to be used in the States?" Condoleezza responded, "I am looking at an order for 5,000, but what I would prefer to do would be to put 100 of these into immediate action, and then discuss whether to buy from you or to buy under licence and we would manufacture." Alan replied, "I understand. I have not patented the product, I believe that it is so sensitive that if we expose the idea in conception it could be copied and developed, etc." "That's alright" said Condoleezza, "We'll look after all of that." Alan asked the Secretary of State for Defence if he really meant whether he would purchase 200 of those fast boats. The Secretary replied, "If they came up to specification, were as fast as that demonstration on the yacht, they were a stealth vessel and carried 30 marines in a fair degree of comfort and were reliable and robust, yes I would purchase 200 – depending on the price of course, but yes." Alan promised, "We will develop a prototype straight away, which will not take long, and when I have demonstrated that, I will let you have a price for 200." With those closing remarks Alan bid them farewell, compliments following him out of the door.

Alan drove straight to the shipyard. He got hold of Gerald and told him about the conversation. Gerald said, "We haven't even discussed that, how did you know I was thinking about it?" Alan said, "Ah, I'm a mind reader! But as far as I am concerned, you can take on as many staff as you like to design the boat but for God's sake get moving – I've told them we wouldn't be long – shall we say three months for a prototype?" "Good God," exclaimed Gerald, "make it four and I'll have a go at it!"

"OK," said Alan, "you realise that is the middle of May?"

Alan then drove round to the lighthouse and told them what had transpired. He wanted a price for 100 and while they were at it, a price for 2,000 and 5,000 units. He went back to his office and rang Andrew McBride. He told Andrew what had happened with both the jobs and he said, "Get hold of Jeremy – get together and form a tight costing system, and come up with some figures of your own – I want those in competition to my other guys."

Andrew grinned, "You're a clever boss you are."

"But make it quick, I want a quote for the President of the United States within 14 days. This must not go cold."

Two weeks later he had competing quotations, one from his accountants and one from Alistair and John. He got all four of them round the table. "Right," he said, "I've had two quotations and they don't agree."

Andrew said, "Well you told us to be independent."

"That's right," said Alan.

"How much are we out?" asked Andrew.

"Actually, it's surprisingly close," said Alan smiling. "The accountants were about 10% higher than the engineers. Will you discuss it and go through the figures together and come up with one quotation? When you've agreed it, draw me up a quotation with full specification details and methods of payment that I can sign and send to America."

They spent the rest of the afternoon in conference and at the end of the day knocked on Alan's door. "We've got a result, we thought we would go more with the accountant's quotation size and let them knock us down. Here's our final figure." Alan looked at it, smiled to himself and signed it. He called his secretary and said, "Get that off to the US Secretary of State." They had put a delivery time of six to eight months for the first 100 and they were working out at £1.5 million each. There was a good margin and good profit, so Alan felt he could form a production line and start producing. A week later he had an order from America signed by the President himself for 100 scanners, as per his quotation.

Alistair and John moved out of the lighthouse and into a spare office in the boatyard and set about designing what was required for the production unit, and the sort of people they wanted on the assembly line. Within a couple of days they had drawn up their plan for a factory – not a large one, as the product was really quite small, and when agreed this was handed to Josh who would do the final designs and get the work done. Alan had plenty of land so they could just get on with it. The total number of employees would be about 20 which was broken down into skilled and unskilled. Some of them would require electronic skills and others electrical and mechanical.

A lot of the components were bought as finished, and John, who was probably the best negotiator, went around to the various supply companies obtaining quotes and telling them that this was just an initial order. He also got them to quote for a further 2,000 at the same time. Two weeks later, when the quotes had come in, they chose who they considered to be the best suppliers at the best price and placed the orders. In the meantime they had been recruiting staff.

It had been a fantastic start to 1997. Alan was totally over the moon that his ideas appeared to be paying off so quickly. Without of course the Lottery money he had won, he could not have developed any of these ideas himself. It took a lot of finance for a one-man show.

CHAPTER 20

It had been a hugely exciting and stimulating 2½ months. Alan had stretched himself and his staff to the limit, so he suggested that they take a week off at Easter and come back refreshed, which they all agreed to do. Alan stood next to his new house. When he had driven the American Secretaries past the house he had noticed that there were chandeliers shining through the windows. When he thought about it, he had not been there since before Christmas, as things had been so hectic.

He went up to the house. Josh was there as usual with Julia. "Well, you've made yourself absent," he said.
"We've had a pretty hectic time," said Alan, "but here I am – let's have a look at what you've done."

The house was finished, all but anyway. It was decorated. Furniture had been bought right the way through the house. Alan loved everything. It was just absolutely brilliant. Julia had made Alan's ideas come through, particularly in his study and in his bedroom.

"When can I move in?" he asked.
"Tomorrow, if you want – we've finished," said Josh.
"Gosh," said Alan, "I didn't think it would happen so quickly."
"I did tell you March," replied Josh.
"Yes, I know, but things drag don't they? I need to get some staff, a butler and a cook. Oh my goodness I'm not going to get any rest over Easter, I can see it!"

Josh asked, "What are we going to do now it is finished?"

Alan said, "Firstly you and Julia take a couple of weeks off, and come back refreshed after Easter. You know the little house facing out to sea on top of the cliffs..."

"That derelict one?" said Josh.

"Yes that's the one. I thought it could be made into something rather special, something that my architect friend would like."

"What architect is that?" he asked.

"Oh his name is err... Josh Bennett I think," Alan laughed.

"Do you mean it?"

"Yes, you and Julia have a look at it, think about it, and if you don't want it that's OK, we'll see if we can find something else, but I thought it might hit the button."

"It will, I know it," said Josh", but I never considered I could afford it."

"Well you can now," said Alan.

He rang his secretary Karen at the boatyard. She had been with him for almost a year. She was a middle-aged lady with ideas that Alan respected. "Karen," he said, "are you very busy?"

She said, "No, not particularly at the moment sir." He asked if she would jump in her car and come up to *Parklands*. He had something he would like to discuss with her.

Twenty minutes later she arrived. She 'oohed' and 'aahed' over the house and thought it was fantastic. Alan said, "I need some help. What do you think? I need a butler, a cook, an upstairs maid, a downstairs maid and maybe somebody else, I don't know."

Karen said, "Yes, I think you need all of those and somebody in the garden as well. I think we'd better go to that top class recruitment agency. It would be better if you could get a husband and wife team. The wife as the cook and the husband as the head gardener, but I think the first person to choose should be the butler who would really be the house manager."

"You're right," replied Alan, "whereabouts are they?"

"Their nearest office is Bristol I think," Karen replied.

"Right, make me an appointment. I need to see them myself."

"When for?"

"Tomorrow, if you can, or the day after".

"OK," said Karen, "I think your house is beautiful, can I have a look round?"

"Of course you can, come on let's have a look".

They went right through the house. They started upstairs with Alan's bedroom. It was quite magnificent. "It should pick up the early morning sun, as well as the south facing view over the lake," Alan explained. It was an impressive room with a dressing room and beautiful en suite. The same could be said for bedroom number two, which was equally impressive, again overlooking the lake and southern aspect of the garden. The other bedrooms were all similar to one another, again beautiful rooms, with en suites, plenty of room and quite staggering views, two of them over the front garden facing north, two of them over the back garden.

Next they went into the servant's area, the butler's rooms – there were three of them, all very impressive. The cook had a smaller bedroom, but still very nice, and then four smaller bedrooms with en suite which were for the junior staff. There were two staircases, one leading down to the main hall, and one down to the corridor in the kitchen and the laundry room. There were also two lifts, one again coming down just off the main hallway and the other again in the same corridor.

They went down the second of them and looked at the kitchen. Karen thought the layout and facilities were fabulous. It faced north over the garden. The laundry room on the south side opened up onto the garden and was shielded from the rest of the garden area by a hedge, which needed of course to grow a little more. There was an impressive pantry next to the kitchen and a sort of boot room. Coming towards the hall, up the corridor was the butler's room, opposite to his wine cellar on the other side of the corridor and then into the dining room. It was an impressive room with a beautiful bow window, beautifully proportioned. There was a table to seat ten people together with ten gorgeous chairs and a side board.

So into the hall, a large room with a big fire place which stood out as the main feature, and all the doors leading off it were in solid oak. The stairs did not come directly into the hall but into a small passage-way. Again, access from the hall was through one of the doors. The lounge was a graceful sedate room where Julia had really put a lot of effort into the colours and it all matched. There were pictures on the wall, two triple-seater settees and two easy chairs, and again one of the main features was the Inglenook fireplace. As before, the bow windows were magnificent.

On the south side it opened up into the sun lounge. Across the hallway straight into a lovely study, with a bow window facing south which was over three metres from end to end. Set into the floor was a three-metre flush stage. The desk and chair were placed on one half of the stage. Backing onto the front of the desk were two reception type armchairs. At the push of a button the desk revolved through 180°, which allowed the occupier to either face across the desk out through the window into the garden or by rotating back 180° he was able to face into the room.

A further door on the side of the study lead into the library which was well equipped with beautiful shelving all the way round. It wasn't over large, but certainly large enough for Alan's books which were still up in Sunderland. He had had all his personal possessions including his books put into storage, as he didn't know where he would be. He made a mental note to get them brought down as soon as possible. Another door off the study led into a little alcove with a toilet, washbasin and a sort of boot and coat hanging space with an outside door to the garden. As you went through the door on the right hand side was the hedge, on the other side of which was the laundry room.

Karen was really impressed. She thought it was the most beautiful house she had ever been in and she had certainly seen quite a bit of life and visited stately homes and other places like that. She said, "I'll get off now and see if I can make an appointment for you for tomorrow".

CHAPTER 21

The following day Alan drove up to Bristol and met up with the recruitment agency. He explained his requirements and the man was most helpful. "I don't see that there is any problem. It is not an uncommon request these days, but I think you should firstly choose the butler, who will be your house manager. Then let him be involved in choosing the cook and the rest of the staff," he said.

Alan replied, "I agree. I'd prefer to employ the butler first. By all means get some cooks and possibly gardener/cook married couple combinations, and as you suggest, I will talk with the butler about the rest of the staff."

"How long have we got?" asked the man from the recruitment agency.

"No time at all," said Alan, "I've moved in today! Well, hopefully I shall do so within the next week or two."

"Give me a couple of weeks," he replied, "I don't want to rush this, I want to make sure you get the right person so that we're not coming back again in three month's time wanting someone new."

"I agree with that sentiment" said Alan.

"What I'll do is select three or four for you to interview"

"Ok," said Alan, "What I would like to do is to interview them here, choose one or at the most two, and then re-interview them at the house so they can see the facility."

"Good idea," said the manager.

Two weeks later Alan was back in the manager's office interviewing, separately of course, four applicants. Eventually he boiled it down to one man in his mid-thirties. He had ten years experience as a butler, and prior to that had been an assistant butler. He was well qualified and came with good references. He said that he was ready for a change from the London scene and wanted to live in the country, which is what had attracted him to the job in the first place. However, he knew that his current employers would not be very pleased if he gave in his notice.

"When are you available to come to the house and look it over?" asked Alan

"I could do that this time next week. Thursday is my day off," the man replied.

"Alright," said Alan, "I tell you what – I'll come and pick you up at Bristol aerodrome and we can fly down. It'll save a couple of hours of your time. Shall we say 10 am?"

"Yes, sir," he replied, "I'll be there."

So it was agreed. His name was Edward Burns, and had been born in 1962. They met up the following week and Alan flew them down to the house, landing for the first time on his drive, which he had asked Josh to make sure was fit to land on. They circled the house and surrounding area, and Edward was most impressed with it. Alan did the tour of the house for the second time, and then they went into his study and spent the next hour talking. He made sure that it was the sort of place that Edward would like to live, pretty way out from everything else. They discussed terms, holidays, pension rights and the whole situation.

At the end of the day Alan said, "If you want the job it's yours."

Edward answered, "Yes please sir."

"When can you start?" asked Alan.

"In four weeks' time, as I have to give notice."

"Ok," said Alan. "Now, about a cook, have you any ideas?"

"No," said Edward, "really none at all. I don't think it would be fair to try and take the cook from my existing employer."

"I agree," said Alan. "Well, keep your eyes and ears open and in the meantime I shall advertise. Perhaps we can contact you so you can be in on the interviews?"

"Oh, I'd like that," said Edward.

Edward then asked, "What about the rest of the staff?"

"Well," said Alan "I have an idea. There are a number of bright children attending the local school. I was with the headmaster the other day and he was saying what a great shame it was that they couldn't go to university because their families could not afford to send them. What I would like to do is to choose a couple of girls, one for upstairs and one for downstairs, 16 years of age, who have got good GCSE results and want to go to university. I will pay them a proper wage for the job they are doing, give them every afternoon and evening off unless they are required for a special event or visitors, and the time would be used for their study. If they are successful with their 'A'-levels, I would sponsor them through their chosen university."

"That is extremely generous," said Edward.

"Well, it seems a shame to me that these children cannot reach their true potential. Hopefully this will give two of them a chance, and if it works out maybe we can repeat this in two years. Do you think you can work this into the house scheme?"

"Oh there is no doubt at all," replied Edward. "They will have plenty of time on their hands quite honestly. What about someone to assist the cook?"

"Well, again I would like to take a girl whose family is desperate for their child to bring in a wage who perhaps is not university material, but would be interested in catering and could take an HND or similar."

"I'm all for that," said Edward, "that sounds a great idea".

Alan flew Edward back to Bristol. He was to start working for Alan on 1st May.

Alan immediately contacted the recruitment agency again. "I need a cook and a head gardener," he said. "I think it would be preferable if they were a husband and wife team. It's a permanent position. The garden is a virgin garden and someone will have to take responsibility for it."

"Alright," said the recruitment agent, "I don't see any problem here. If we select three couples for you to interview would that be alright?"

"Certainly," said Alan. "What I'd like to do is to come up to Bristol, interview them and then select the ones I like and ask them to come down to my house at Eden Stanton."

"That's fine," he said, "when are you wanting to take them on?"

"Immediately," Alan replied, "the very earliest possible time."

"OK, we'll contact you within the next week or two."

Two weeks later the recruitment agency rang Alan. "We are having difficulty getting hold of a husband and wife team. We have only got one such couple and they seem to be ideal, but we can't offer you a choice of people as we usually like to do."

"When can they start?"

"Well that's the point," said the recruitment agency, "this couple could start immediately."

"I'll come up and interview them" said Alan. With that, three days later he was interviewing George and Betty Hetherington. Alan had managed to contact Edward and arranged for him to be at the interview as well.

They were both in their mid-thirties and seemed very fit. George seemed to be rather over qualified as a gardener, as he had got a good degree from a horticultural college. He explained that his father had brought him up, as his mother had died giving birth. He lived in the Black Country around Stoke. His father was insistent that his boy would live in the country so he took him out into the fields as much as possible. As he grew older, his father had him work on a local farm during the holidays. His father had worked extremely hard and had saved in order to put George through college. Eventually

George had gone to a horticultural college and had passed with flying colours.

He had, however, felt that farming was not the right area for him, and wanted something with more finesse. He had joined one of the country houses as deputy head gardener and had five happy years. Then he decided that he ought to be head gardener himself. He had gone to this house in Beeston as head gardener when he was 33 years old and had been there a couple of years when Betty had joined the staff in the kitchen. She was to be head cook. He immediately took a fancy to Betty and they started going out on their free day. Eventually the mistress of the house found out and said that fraternisation with another employee was not allowed. If they persisted, they would be dismissed. George and Betty were so aggrieved at this that they both handed in their noticed and had left Beeston just over a week ago.

Betty had a somewhat different tale. She was an orphan and did not know her father or her mother at any time. She had initially gone to an orphanage and then to a number of foster parents. She was a bit of a rebel and had not settled down very well to being fostered. At the age of 16 she had basically been thrown out on the street and had to cater and look after herself. This proved to be a great shock, and for a while she lived rough. Fortunately, however she did not get into the drugs scene, and eventually got a job as a scullery maid in a large house. The head cook was very vicious to her, but she was getting fed and had a little amount of money.

Within two years she moved to another house as an upstairs maid and there they treated her much better. She was paid a reasonable rate for the job but she decided that her future lay in the kitchen. She liked the idea of cooking, although she had done very little. She realised that she would need to have a qualification. She saved and saved over the next six years, read books on cookery, watched the cook whenever she could, and helped with the laying of the dining table and made herself very useful. She managed to get on a Cordon

Bleu cookery course on her one day off per week which continued for two years. Eventually Betty saw an advertisement for an assistant cook and applied for it. She got the job, had five years in this post before moving again as head cook at Beeston.

George and Betty had been married only four days before Alan interviewed them. He had taken to this well qualified couple and it seemed that they were absolutely ideal for the position that he had available. Alan asked Edward if he had any questions to which he replied, "No, everything has been covered." So Alan asked them to wait outside and conferred with Edward. They both agreed that this couple seemed to be ideal and called them back in.

Alan had flown up to Bristol to see them. "I am going to suggest something that I have never done before. I have not interviewed anybody else for this job. It is an important job, but what I would like to suggest is that you come back with me now in my aeroplane, have a look at the house. As it is getting a bit late you could spend the night in the house if you wish. If you like it, I will offer you the jobs." George replied, "From what you have described the jobs would suit us very well. Since we have very little baggage or luggage with us, could we pack a suitcase and bring that with us? Then if all is agreeable we could stay – if not, then there is really nothing lost." Alan thought for a moment. "Yes, OK. Where are your things?" "We rented some digs until we got married. It will really only take us about 15 minutes to gather up our things, pay our rent and be ready." "Well, I'll wait here for you."

They shook hands and after a few brief words with the recruitment agency manager, Alan had a cup of coffee and waited. About 15 minutes later George and Betty came back with a suitcase each. Alan ordered a taxi and they went off to the airport. Alan flew them back to Eden Stanton, landing on his own drive. He had practised landing by himself two or three times and there had been no problem. His drive was perfect – in fact, far better than the average landing strip for light aircraft.

Alan showed them around the house and Betty was absolutely over-aught by the kitchen – it was the most wonderful kitchen she had ever seen. He had asked Josh to meet him at the house and he was there waiting. Josh took George around the estate in his Land Rover and when they came back after about half-an-hour George was really enthusiastic. "This is a virgin garden, this is everything I have ever dreamed about," he said. "It's wonderful!"

"Well, I'd like you to confer with both Josh here and his good lady Julia, they both have had considerable time with the house and I'm sure they will have some valuable input into the garden layout."
"Oh," said George, "the more help I can get the better".
Alan said, "Please bear in mind that I do want one, possible two herd of deer, but we can talk about all that later. Take your cases up to the bedroom. I'll show you through, and we'll talk about it when we've had something to eat."
"Have you any food in the kitchen?" Betty asked.
Alan said, "Oh yes there is some food that Julia managed to get for me."
"Well could I have a look and I'll cook us a meal?" asked Betty.
"OK," said Alan. An hour later the three of them sat down and enjoyed a hearty evening meal.

After they had finished Alan said "What do you think?"
"We are totally over the moon, both of us," George replied, "we would very much like the job."
"It's yours" said Alan.
George and Betty hugged each other.
"We haven't discussed accommodation or anything"
"No," said George "But that is secondary to us."
"Well," said Alan, "we are creating three houses within the Home Farm buildings and I know Josh is working on the design of these. However, I think it will be at least six to twelve months before they are completed. The only other accommodation is internal in this house, which is basically the cook's bedroom with sitting-room –

unless you have any other suggestions you could use that in the meantime."

"That's fine," said George, "absolutely fine."

"Don't you want to look at the planned house?" asked Alan.

"Oh we can look at that later on," said George.

Alan agreed to pay them slightly more than they had previously been paid. He explained too that Edward would be joining them as butler and house manager. He was responsible for everything inside the house. He told them about his plans for the additional staff and they both thought that was a wonderful idea. George said, "I think we might need more than the three of us, however, to get the garden into shape."

"Oh," said Alan, "I think you will have to bring in outside contractors, but I'll leave that with you and Josh to sort out."

They retired contented to their beds.

Edward had told Alan that he had handed in his notice to his previous employer who had more or less told him to go straight away so he would be able to join them the next week if that was alright. Alan of course was delighted.

Retiring to bed that night Alan could not believe how in such a short space of time he had managed to get what he thought was a first-class butler, a first-class cook and a first-class head gardener. He must get on with the other junior staffing as soon as possible.

The next few days he was totally tied up with business and it was not until the following Monday that he was able to telephone the headmaster of the school and go and see him. Alan had his idea put onto paper and when he showed this to the headmaster, he was delighted.

He said, "Yes, as I said we have a number of students that would fit the bill, both boys and girls, and I think this is a wonderful opportunity. The only way you can select them is to interview them yourself.

Alan said, "I wonder if it is possible to sort of interview them without them knowing, to perhaps see them in class and talk to them in class?"

"That's a good idea," said the headmaster, "why don't I bring together all the GCSE year – there will be about 50 pupils there and I think we'd better wait until they've completed their exams." This was agreed.

Some weeks later the headmaster rang Alan to say he had organised an opportunity for him to talk to the GCSE group. They arranged a date and on the appointed day Alan went up to the school. He started by asking how the GCSE examinations had gone. There was not much feedback as they were all hoping but nobody knew any results yet. Alan then moved onto what they were all going to do. He went along the front row and talked about various universities and the particular subjects they wanted to do. Some of them said they wanted to be a lawyer, or a doctor, or similar.

Along the second row there was a girl that when Alan asked her which university she hoped to go to she said, "I'm not going to university. I'm going to get a job instead."

Alan said, "OK."

She replied, "I'd like to have gone to university but my parents can't afford it, and I need to bring some money into the household."

"I see," said Alan. "Anybody else in that position?"

A boy put his hand up. "Yes," he said, "I'm exactly the same. I would have liked to have gone to university, to horticultural college to be a farmer."

"Is your father in the agricultural business?" Alan asked.

"Yes," said the boy, "he's a farm labourer."

Another boy stuck up his hand. "I'm in the same position. My father is out of work at the moment and I have three young brothers. My mother died a year ago."

And so it went on. Out of the 55 students that were in the room, Alan discovered that 20-odd were not going on to university and of those, twelve would like to have done so but their parents couldn't afford to let them go, even if it had been free at the university. Alan had asked his secretary Karen to come along to the meeting and as each of the children spoke, he asked them to first of all announce their name. Knowing what he was looking for, Karen was able to identify the twelve students, four girls and eight boys. She had also drawn a plan of the rows of children and indicated where the twelve where with their names on the plan.

So Alan chose four girls and four of the boys to interview. He asked the headmaster and Edward and George to be present at the interviews. Between them they selected two girls and two boys. One of the girls was to work as an upstairs maid and the other as a downstairs maid. Both the two boys were to work in the garden.

However, he had still not selected some help for the kitchen. The headmaster pointed him in the direction of one young lady he felt would fit the bill. Alan interviewed her and went round to see her parents. They were delighted as although she wasn't 'behind the door', neither was she university material. Certainly Alan felt that she could do an HND in cookery and develop from there. Later he went round to see the two girls with Edward and the two boys with George. There were one or two awkward moments, but in the main the parents were pleased, as well they should, since their children were being offered a normal wage for a normal job, but with the opportunity for a large amount of time off to study. Subject to obtaining the right level of 'A'-levels, they would also get sponsorship through university. It was a very fine offer indeed.

CHAPTER 22

By 1st July everyone had started and was in position. The house was buzzing with activity, as was the garden. Through Josh, George had managed to get a good contractor and Josh had drawn up the plans for the major parts of the garden. One of the first things that he did was to put a good strong electric fence running the entire length from the road to the house from the north side of the driveway. This was to house the deer herd.

Alan had been looking around and learning about deer for some time, and the girl who ran the riding school had actually worked in a deer park and had quite a lot of experience. She advised Alan who to contact, and before long he was offered a herd. Josie came with him to inspect them together with a local vet that they used for the horses. They were a splendid herd, and although originally established over 500 years ago, there was nothing wrong with them at all. The price was extremely reasonable and Alan had them brought over by road transport and put into their 'enclosure'.

In June Gerald rang in and said he would like a meeting with regard to problems on the boat. They were experiencing difficulties with the servo mechanisms right through the boat. These were all electronically computer driven and it was a very complicated design. Apart from the water pads on each side of boat which were retracted or lowered depending on speed and weather and water conditions, the engines were phased with the level of the boat. The sails were all operated through servo mechanism and coupled with the avoidance computer system, which again operated all of these systems.

Alan asked Gerald if he was really out of his depth with it. The answer of course was, "Yes."

"We need to get some outside consultants," said Alan.

"Yes, I've looked at one or two and there is one company that stands out in this field. They are a London based company and I think you've got to get them on fast. There is a lot hanging on this."

A week later Gerald reported that a lady from the consultancy would be arriving the following day. She was called Susan Strange and she was an expert in the field. Alan's heart missed a beat leap – could it be the Susan Strange, his one time girlfriend, the love of his life? He had never stopped thinking about her and all these years had gone by.

A few days passed. Gerald said that the consultant on the servo mechanism had spent two days with them and felt that she had a clear way forward for them to operate. She needed another couple of days to put her ideas on paper, but considered there could be a very satisfactory outcome. Alan said, "Why don't you and Jim come along for dinner and bring this lady with you. How about tonight?"

"That's OK with me," said Gerald, "I'll see about the other two." He rang back shortly afterwards saying that was alright with the other two, would seven o'clock do."

Alan suddenly realised he had given his staff no warning at all. Hurriedly he got Edward to rally the team and seven o'clock arrived. Alan let them in. His heart was pounding. Could it really be his Susan?

In she walked. She looked gorgeous. Alan immediately noticed that there was not ring on her finger. "Hello, Susan. It's really lovely to see you after all this time."

She was rather taken aback, "Alan what are you doing... ?"

Alan replied, "I didn't know whether it was you or not to be honest, I just saw the name, but I really am pleased to see you. I hope that you'll accept my hospitality."

"Of course," said Susan, "we were meeting the boss of the whole outfit tonight."

"Yes," said Alan, "that's me. It's my company, it's my boatyard. Don't you remember?"

"And this is your house, I suppose?"

"Yes," said Alan, "you are actually the first visitors here. I've only just finished building it."

"Were those deer we saw on the right hand side of the drive as we came through?"

"Yes," said Alan. "I have just acquired them. Aren't they gorgeous?"

"Wow," she said, "you've certainly come up in the world. What happened to your wife?"

Alan replied, "We're divorced. I have two beautiful children. What about you, are you married?"

"No," said Susan, "I was, but we got divorced. Fortunately I didn't have any children."

Mrs Hetherington, as she preferred to be addressed (rather than 'Betty'), had cooked a fabulous meal. Main course was leg of lamb, and there was a wonderful starter and sweet. The wines that Edward served were really perfectly chosen and delicious. It was a first-class meal in every way. Susan explained how she felt the servo mechanism could be simplified, and she had nearly completed the design for a new system. She really had worked very fast and appeared to know exactly what she was doing. Alan thanked her on behalf of the team and he managed to get a few words in private and asked if he could take her out for dinner somewhere. Susan agreed.

"I'm here tomorrow, but after that I'm back in London."

"Well, let me pick you up at the yard, about five or six o'clock?"

"Six o'clock," replied Susan.

Alan could hardly wait for six o'clock the following evening to come. He kept marching up and down and couldn't think straight. "Oh dear, am I in love again?" he thought.

They went out for dinner that night. Alan had chosen an hotel some distance away. It was a good hotel and the food was excellent. It was quite obvious from the outset that Susan was not the girl she was when they parted 21 years previously. Life had not treated her too kindly and Alan felt that in a way she blamed him for walking out on her. By the end of the evening it was obvious that there was no point in pursuing the relationship. Susan made it perfectly clear that she was no longer interested. Her life was in London, that's what she enjoyed and what she wanted. They parted as Alan dropped her off at her hotel, best of friends, each wishing the other all the best for the future. So that was the end of that.

CHAPTER 23

A week later if was Judd Court's turn to ring Alan with a problem. Judd of course was the manager of Home Farm and it was very rarely that he contacted Alan – it was usually the other way about. They had their monthly meeting and everything was going well. Judd explained that he was having trouble with the farmer in the neighbouring farm. "He swears that he has a right-of-way over our property. I contacted the solicitors and they came back saying they had looked at the deeds and there was no right of way. This bloke, Jim Giles, is an old man and I am at my wits end with him."

Alan said he would go and see him. Jim was really quite subservient. He was an old man, Alan guessed in his 70s. "What' the problem?" Alan asked.

"Well," said Jim, "this farm has been in my family for five generations. My great-grandfather sold a strip of land to the railways in order for them to build a railway line. It actually left one very large field, over 50 acres, with no access. Great-grandfather did a deal with the Lord of the Manor who owned Home Farm to give him access to this field and this you understand was for a consideration. The deeds I know were not altered – neither mine, nor his, but I've never had any problem up until now. They have always left a strip unploughed for me to gain access."

"Your story rings true to me," Alan said, "you won't have any problem with access from us."

"You're a gentleman," replied Jim, "but he's ploughed it up."

"Then you'll have to walk over the ploughed land."

"OK, that's no problem."

"Have you no wife and family?" Alan asked.

"My wife died three years back, we have no children. I had two boys – one went to Canada and the other to Australia, and I've not seen them for a long time." Jim replied.

"Look," said Alan, "if we can help you in any way we will. If you ever want to sell your farm I'd be interested to buy it. Here's my card. If you want to contact me, give me a ring."

When Alan got back he rang the solicitors and asked for the deeds for Home Farm to be sent over. When these arrived he poured over them and with a bit of help from Josh they found that taking over Jim Giles's farm would make absolute sense as it would make a perfect combination of the two farms. It also gave them considerable opportunity to develop their housing programme.

Alan noticed a dot and a 'C' and he asked, "What's that?"

"It's an island," Josh explained.

"What's it on my Deeds for?"

"Well, presumably you own the island."

"I don't know anything about that," said Alan. "Will you come with me and have a look this weekend?"

"Of course" Josh replied.

So at the weekend Alan, Bill, Edward, Josh and Julia set out in their hire boat and sailed to the map reference where the island should be. It was a good 20 miles off shore, west south west of the lighthouse. The island was obviously uninhabited. Sheer cliffs rose out of the sea, 20ft-30ft high, with no chance of getting to the top unless you were a real climber. There was obviously vegetation and the island when they circled it, was approximately one mile in width and two miles in length, so quite a large island.

They moved from the east side of the island around the north and down the west and were on the point of coming home when Josh cried out, "Look, look! There's a cove in there!" They carefully made their way through a narrow gap in the rocks. They were using the echo sounder all the time, but there seemed to be plenty of water under the keel. They squeezed through the rock and the cove became quite a large enclosed bay, with a sandy beach about 10m or 12m in depth and then more or less a forest behind it.

As they went in very slowly watching the echo sounder, Edward cried out, "Look, look in the water!" There were two black boys, naked, who as they saw them they rushed out of the water up the beach and disappeared into the trees. "Well," said Alan, "what next?!" They got into the middle of the bay and dropped anchor. They lowered the dinghy and Edward, who always carried a gun just to be prepared, brought it with him = although Alan said, "OK, but hide it." The two of them rowed ashore with Julia, leaving the others on the boat.

Alan shouted as loud as possible, "Please, we're only friends, we didn't know you were here, it's no problem please come and talk to us." After quite a while a black man appeared out of the forest area. He was a middle-aged man, scantily clad and he held his hands high above his head. Alan said, "Please, please put your hands down, we are not going to hurt you."

The man threw himself on the sand and started to cry. Alan went to him and took his hand in his and shook it. "My name is Alan Brown what's yours?"
"Amani Murray," said the man. "We were shipwrecked and swam to this island a long time ago. I managed to save my wife and we have the two boys that you saw."
"Did you have the two boys while you were on the island?" asked Alan.
"Yes" replied Amani.
"Well congratulations," said Alan, "they look fine boys." Amani beamed. He obviously spoke and understood English very well.

Alan said, "You are very welcome here. You have obviously been here a long time and have managed to exist and live here and raise a family. You are very welcome to stay or if you would like to come to the mainland we would be pleased to take you and help you get a job."

Amani said, "Very kind of you, sir, I would like you to meet my wife Kizzy," and he called out, "Kizzy, Kizzy." An attractive middle-aged woman came out from behind the trees, slowly at first, and then she ran to her husband. "It's alright dear, alright," he assured her, "they are friendly." Alan put his hand out. Kizzy took it and fell to the ground. "It's alright," said Amani.

Alan said "Are we the first people that you have seen in how long, 20 years is it?"

Kizzy replied, "For 21 years we have never seen a soul, you are the first. Is it your island?"

"Yes it is" said Alan "You are very welcome to stay here or we would be pleased to take you to the mainland if you would like. Look, you've been here 20 years, why don't you have a good think and a talk and we will come back again in a week's time. I would like if possible to use your beach and have a BBQ if the weather is nice."

Amani replied, "The weather is always nice here, it is beautiful, come I'll show you our house," and he led the way through the trees.

About 25m into the forest stood a house. There was no doubt about it. It was a wooden house, two stories, with two goats tethered underneath ad some steps leading up. "Come on, come on," he said going up the steps of the house. Inside was divided into rooms, and they were in a living room with a veranda that looked out to the sea which they could see between and over the treas.

"Would you like a cup of tea?" asked Kizzy

"That's very nice, thank you" replied Alan. She served tea in no time at all in coconut shells. Alan said "This is very good, it tastes like real tea."

"It is," said Amani, "there was tea growing on the island, believe it or not."

"Good heavens," said Alan, "what else have you discovered here?"

"Well, there are coconuts, as you can see, and there are all sorts of berries and fruits, which we have experimented with. There is a sort of potato that is very nice mashed up. There are quite a number of different wild animals. There's wild pig which you have to be very careful with, very vicious, and some large turkeys. In fact everything you want really to live, except people" said Amani.

"Where are the boys?" asked Alan

Amani went out onto the balcony "Sekou, Gamal, Sekou, Gamal." The two boys appeared, "Come on, it's alright."

They came upstairs and into the room. Alan put his hand out. "Alan," he said.

"Sekou," said the boy.

"Gamal," said the other.

They shook hands all round.

Alan said, "It has been a pleasure to meet you. I'm glad that we have. You are very welcome, as I said, to stay here. We will see you in a week's time, all being well that is."

Amani bowed slightly, "Thank you, sir," he said, "it is a pleasure to meet you also."

And with that Alan, Edward and Julia went back to the boat. They told the others all about it. It really was truly amazing.

"If the weather is nice next Sunday I am going to bring the girls, George and Betty and the boys, and will have a BBQ and spend most of the day here. It is the most beautiful spot. Edward, I want to make it clear that we must not leave any mess whatsoever. The sand must be as clean as it is when we saw it today."

"I understand," said Edward.

CHAPTER 24

The following week Alan had a phone call from Jim Giles "Do you still want to buy my farm?" He asked.

"Of course," replied Alan.

"Can we talk about it?"

"Would you prefer to come to my house or shall I come to yours?" Alan asked.

"I can come round tomorrow morning," Jim said, "if that's convenient."

"Very good," said Alan. "What time?"

"About ten o'clock."

"That's alright," said Alan.

The next day at 10.00am Jim turned up. He had all the deeds of his property with him, and a valuation that had been done just a year before by a well-known valuer. Alan looked at the price. "Is this the price you want? He asked.

"Yes," said Jim.

"Well then I would like to buy it," said Alan "but…"

"But?" said Jim.

"What are you going to do?"

"I don't know. That is a big problem."

"Well," said Alan, "I am converting three properties at Home Farm into houses, but they won't be ready for another six months. If you like you can stay in your own property for that time and we will work around you. There will be no rent to pay, but you would have to pay for your own costs and when the house is ready you can buy it from me or rent it. However, first you will need to look at it."

"That's a very kind offer," said Jim, "I would like to look at the plans and see where the house will be."

"Of course," said Alan, "I'll get Judd to show you round."

"Oh I don't like that man," said Jim.

"Oh come along, Jim, he's quite harmless really. He's a nice guy, and now we've settled our differences, I'm sure he will be very obliging. I think he'll also be delighted when he knows he's going to have some extra land to look after."

"OK," said Jim. So they slapped hands and Alan got his lawyers to work at once.

The following week had been gorgeous and when Sunday arrived it was a beautiful day. Twelve of them piled onto the yacht. Alan told them all to bring their swimming costumes, sun lotion and towels and to be prepared for a super day out. So Alan was joined by Bill, Suzanne and Catherine (who had turned up for the weekend), Edward, George, Betty, the three girls (Bridget, Jean and Gill) and Gerard and William. Unfortunately Josh and Julia had arranged to visit some friends that weekend, but perhaps it was as well as the boat was very crowded.

They set out and sailed slowly, reaching the island just under two hours later. The girls gasped as they entered the bay. It really was a most wonderful sight – it was like a Caribbean island suddenly springing out of the Channel and Irish Sea. They anchored making several trips between shore to deposit everyone and all their paraphernalia. Some of them actually jumped or dived in from the boat and swam ashore. It was idyllic, and within a few minutes they were joined by Amani, Sekou and Gamal. Alan of course invited them to join his party for the BBQ. He told them, "We are going to have loads of lovely rich things, that no doubt you will have missed over the years."

It took some time before the homemade BBQ fire was burning properly and suitable for cooking on. They soon had chicken, sausages, pieces of steak, lamb cutlets and chops. This was all supplemented with baked potatoes which took rather a long time but were worth waiting for.

In the meantime most people, in particular the youngsters, were swimming and having a wonderful time in the bay. Alan, and of course Edward, supervised the cooking of the BBQ. After they had finished eating most basked in the sun and some fell asleep.

Amani asked Alan if he could have a word and they moved to his house in the trees. Amani said, "I have something to tell you that I've not told anyone, not even my two boys. You see," he said, "Kizzy and I are not really married. We intended to get married, she was only 17 when we were shipwrecked, and of course once on the island here we couldn't get married so we had a little private ceremony and have lived as husband and wife."

"Well," said Alan, "there is certainly nothing to be ashamed of and I think it can easily be rectified if you wish. You could get married on the mainland and this could either be done in secret, or involve the whole family, which I think would be a better idea."

Amani replied, "Do you really think we could get married?"

"Of course," said Alan, "I can't see any problems at all."

"That would be wonderful. It is such a major thing with Kizzy. I think she would be over the moon when I tell her."

Alan asked, "Have you thought any more about the talk that we had last week?"

"Oh yes," replied Amani, "we would like to come back with you if that were possible, all four of us. We feel that the boys need education we can't give them. It already might be a bit too late. Kizzy and are so happy on this island, just the two of us, and we feel that unless our ideas change we would like to come back here and live if that is possible?"

"There is no problem in anything that you have suggested," said Alan. "You can come over and spend a week or a month and see whether you like it and if the boys can settle down. I will get them into the local school and find you somewhere to live, and if you want to do some work when you are over there I know that my head gardener, George, would be delighted to have the extra help at the moment."

"Oh thank you, thank you so much," said Amani.

"However, there is just one problem. We are so loaded with people on the yacht we really haven't got room to take another four people back, so we'll come over tomorrow and pick you up. This will give you time to put a few bits and pieces together and to shut up your house for the time being."

"Oh thank you, thank you again," said Amani, "we are so grateful to you."

Alan said, "You have really no need, I have not done anything for you as yet."

They wandered back to the beach where people were beginning to stir. The young ones were back in the water playing with a football they had found. The two black boys, Sekou and Gamal were joining in the fun. They were of course excellent swimmers and had very strong muscular bodies. The girls were quite taken with them.

After a while Alan said to Edward, "I think we should get back. It will take us a couple of hours and it's already four o'clock."

"Ok," said Edward, "everyone get back to the yacht we're going home."

Alan went across to Amani and Kizzy. "We will come out to you tomorrow, it'll probably be round about midday if that's alright, unless the weather turns extremely bad, but please expect us."

Kizzy said, "Thank you so much, you are very kind to us."

"Don't worry about anything," said Alan, "see you tomorrow."

With that he got on the last dinghy that was going back to the yacht, motored out of the bay and set sail for home. They had had a truly wonderful day. Everyone was really quite tired and one by one all the people on the boat came to him and thanked him for a fantastic day. Alan just sat and thought about the wonder of it, how extremely fortunate they all were to just have an island like that appear as it were to be presented for their own personal use. It was just too good to be true. He vowed to have some research done into what the island was called, as there was certainly no name on the deeds. Alan named it there and then – Murray Island, after Amani and Kizzy. "Murray Island it will be," said Alan, "whether it has been previously named or not, I shall have it put on the deeds as Murray Island."

The following day Alan, Josh and Edward took the yacht out back to Murray Island. They picked up George and Kizzy and the two boys. Alan had been able to rent the house that he had moved out of only a bit earlier that year. It would be ideal for them, for a short while anyway, until they found their feet on the mainland. He took them straight down to the house where Mrs Hetherington and the girls had been busy all day and had filled the fridge with food and left instructions on how to operate everything. They had really done a splendid job. Amani and Kizzy were absolutely delighted. Sekou and Gamal felt rather nervous and wondered what was going to happen next. Alan had spoken with the headmaster and he wanted to meet up with the boys the next day. "I will ask Edward to come down at 10am and take you and the boys up to the school."

Alan returned to his home at *Parklands* and rang the local vicar and asked him to come and see him. He turned up that evening and Alan discreetly told him about Amani and Kizzy. The vicar explained that there was no problem at all, and he could marry them discreetly or they could have a larger wedding if they wished. Alan wrote a handwritten letter to Amani about what the vicar had told him and confirmed it was really up to them as to how they wished to proceed. He gave it to Edward to take down the following morning.

CHAPTER 25

Alan's yacht, *Endeavour* was ready. They had completed all the sea trials, and the new systems worked perfectly. Alan raced straight down to the boatyard. He went over the yacht and it really was a beautiful sailing boat. He turned to Gerald and said "What about doing the 'Around Britain and Ireland Yacht Race', it's about four weeks off? It would give us a huge amount of publicity." Gerald was not sure, but promised to look into it.

The Around Britain Race is about 2,000 miles long. It starts from Cowes on the Isle of Wight and goes right around the UK and Ireland, coming back again round the Solent to Cowes. One of the qualifications of the race, the toughest in the Northern Hemisphere, is that at least half the crew have to have raced 500 miles. Gerald of course would qualify and with all the equipment that they had on board, a two man crew would be good enough.

A few days later Gerald told Alan that he thought it was an excellent idea. He had been in contact with the organisers and they were delighted that he would be entering a new boat. He had recruited three friends, so there were four of them, three of which had done a considerable amount of racing, including of course Gerald himself. He had invited them down for the following weekend to have a test run on *Endeavour*. They would have to move very fast and get the boat fully equipped and ready for the race in order to set off the end of the first week in August.

The race starts in the Eastern Solent, along the south coast towards Land's End, across the Irish Sea to the south west corner of Ireland, and then the fleet proceed north to the Hebrides, passing St. Kilda and then heading out towards the Shetland Isles. Back around the most northern point of the UK and then across the top of Scotland and down the North Sea, the journey passes the oil rigs and right down to the Dover Straights and then back along the south coast to Cowes on the Isle of Wight. A race of this hardness would test any boat and so Alan hoped that they would win the race, gain the publicity and hopefully a few orders would follow.

A few weeks later and the race started, they were off! Gerald had worked tirelessly to get the boat ready – this was a real test for it. The race can take well over a week to complete, even for the fastest boats. Gerald and the *Endeavour* came sailing in up the Solent only three days after setting out. It was a record, they were first by a very long way and he couldn't believe it – the organisers had not even prepared the finishing line. Here he was with big accolades splashed across the newspapers and the news the next day – *Endeavour* was a star! The enquiries flooded in and several orders were placed within 24 hours. It had been a major success and put the yacht on the market.

CHAPTER 26

Alan had an important meeting with Gerald and Jim Caldwell, the production manager. He told Gerald that he had to pass everything over to Jim, and Jim had to take over the production of the yacht. The quality control system had to be tight and initially little deviation would be allowed from the standard. Gerald of course had to concentrate now on the stealth boat – complete the design and get it into production. It would need a new factory, as 200 had already been ordered and there were many more potential orders in the pipeline. Alan asked Jim to ensure that he had one or two good production managers following him who could take over one or other of the plants. They were under a lot of pressure to produce these highly sophisticated craft in the shortest possible time.

Alan had a meeting with his accountants later that day. They thought that his company should run their first year to 31st December. Alan informed them that he had registered and called the company Cornwall Enterprises Ltd, and that he would like to draw all the enterprises under that global title from an accounting point of view. Each would have its own name of course – there was already Cornish Builders and Scientific Developments Ltd. Everything was agreed and organised.

Judd arrived back from his short holiday and Alan informed him the outcome of his discussions with Jim Giles. Judd of course was delighted to take over another farm. He said he could do with some assistance, as had already been discovered. Alan agreed and suggested that he got a well trained farmer. They had to wait to take over the farm of course, until the lawyers had settled everything, but Judd said he would go round to Jim and make his peace and discuss who was to do what over the next few weeks.

The next evening Alan went to see Amani and Kizzy. They had now been on the mainland for three weeks. Amani had been working for the last two weeks, and working very hard too, in Alan's garden. This allowed him to pay him a living wage. Whilst they were both enjoying the time on the mainland and everyone had been extremely kind, they decided they would like to return to 'their island', as they put it. "What about the boys?" asked Alan.
"Well, the headmaster says that they are both pretty smart. Sekou is 16 and would have to work extremely hard to get his GCSEs within a year. On the other hand, Gamal at 14 has a much better chance of doing things in the normal way."

They had enrolled both boys at the school and both were enjoying school life already and making friends. There did not seem to be any racial prejudice, in fact quite the reverse – other boys and girls wanted to know all about the shipwreck and their island life.

Alan said, "Right then, that's your decision, that's fine and I'm happy to go along with it. However, in order to make your life a little bit more comfortable, I would like you to make a list – a 'wish list' of the things that you would like on the island, practical things. Perhaps you could do with some better means of heating water, a cooker of some sort for food, maybe a small boat to go fishing, some tools, fishing nets, etc.? Above all I would like to have a communication system between Edward in the house and yourselves on the island, and this can be quite simply organised. I will get Edward to look into it. But if there is anything you can think of that you would like to take back with you, please let me know and we will try and organise it."
Kizzy said, "Oh you are too good, you really are, there is one thing I loved here and that's the beds."

A couple of weeks later Edward, Josh and the two boys, Gerald and William, took Amani and Kizzy back to the Murray Island. They were loaded up with all sorts of gear – hens, a cow that had just given birth (so they had milk), and many other things to make their life more comfortable. In order to get everything to the island Edward had had to hire a small cargo vessel – it was an open ship and well used to this type of transportation. The weather was good and they had no problem in landing the Murrays and seeing them settled in. Somehow or other they found a method of communicating with them using wireless technology. It was a one-to-one system that operated in both directions, either from the island or from *Parklands*.

The girls in the house and Suzanne were all asking when they could go back to the island. They had enjoyed their visit so much. So they all went back the following Sunday and again had a wonderful BBQ. While they were there Amani came across and talked to Alan. He said, "It is very strange, but I do believe that there are other people on this island. Do you know we have been here for about 20 years and I have never seen anybody? The last few years I have felt that there is someone else on the island, particularly when I have walked towards the middle of it, but I never really looked very closely or tried to find anyone. It's just a sense, a feeling that I have."

Alan said "There don't appear to be any charts of the waters around the island, nor indeed any plan of the island itself or what's on the island. I think we should try and investigate. Let's try and do it before the end of the summer holidays – the boys could join in and the girls. Perhaps, Amani, you would take charge of the expedition?"

So it was agreed and two weeks later they set out. Amani was in charge with his two boys Sekou and Gamal, the two boys from the garden, Gerard Bolton and William. The plan was to chart the island as they went over it. The two girls, Jean and Gill went with them. They were to take samples of the flora and plant life and they also took an anthropologist Alan had met at a dinner a few months previously. He was very keen to look at the flora and also the mineral that was on the island. In all there were eight of them.

The plan was to go up the east side of the island first and then come down the west. They had radios that would allow them to report in each evening as to how they had progressed. Amani said that the plan to explore the island would take not more than seven days. Gerard and William had taken their instructions to chart the island seriously, and they had read up on what was needed. They had also spoken to the anthropologist who they felt would be able to help them with the task. They had got together a limited amount of equipment and felt that they could do a worthwhile job. The girls, Jean and Gill had also been down to the library and had tried to learn as much as they could about how to collect specimen plants and so on. Alan felt that the whole exercise was becoming a really worthwhile opportunity. He kept in contact every evening and followed their progress as Edward positioned them on a rough map that he had drawn of the island.

It was on the fifth day of the expedition that they rang Edward round about midday to say that they had found two women, on the island. They were French, healthy and in good condition. At first they had been very frightened. Gradually they had been able to tell them that they were friends and were there to help them. Apparently they had been shipwrecked on the island for a number of years.

Amani had decided that he would split his troop the following day. Sekou, together with William and Gill, would accompany the two French women back to Amani's house on the island. Alan and Edward decided that they would go out the following day and see what the situation was.

Alan and Edward got to the island in the middle of the afternoon. Kizzy had prepared a very nice BBQ and was expecting everybody back by about four o'clock. Alan was introduced to the French lady, Madame Chantal de Vivier, and her daughter Avril. Apparently they had been on the island for about 5 years. They had been shipwrecked and somehow had managed to get to a small beach on the west of the island and then through a cave to the top of the island. They had lived off the land perfectly comfortably. Her daughter was now 13 and they were beginning to wonder whether they would ever get back to civilisation. The young girl seemed quite happy just playing in the water, swimming and playing with the other teenagers.

The mother seemed a little over aught and was still having difficulty recognising that they had been 'rescued'. Alan had a quiet word with her and told her not to worry – that he would see them back to the mainland and find them some accommodation. The woman asked if he thought it would be possible that she could get a job perhaps teaching French or something. Alan was quite surprised at this, as he thought she would want to go straight back to France, but he readily agreed and thought that there was a good possibility of getting a job at a local school. Apparently she had been an English teacher in France. Something, however, was not quite as it seemed, and Alan kept pondering as to what was wrong. However, they had a good BBQ and everyone departed back to *Parklands* on the yacht and a power boat.

The de Viviers stayed overnight at *Parklands* and next morning Alan took them down to the cottage that he had previously rented and installed them. He then arranged with the headmaster for both the girl and her mother to go and meet up with him at eleven o'clock that morning. He explained what had happened and what they were up to. He suggested that they should take things easy as school didn't start for another two weeks.

Edward took them both up to the school and after the headmaster had had a good discussion with both Mme de Vivier and her daughter, he agreed that they could take the girl into the school and was delighted that he had found a good French teacher. Both would start at the beginning of the following term. Alan had suggested that they perhaps might like to do some shopping and buy some clothes and essentials, which of course they had not had for the past 5 years. He also suggested that they joined him for dinner that night. When they came to the house, Chantal de Vivier was gushing in her thanks to Alan for all the help that he had given them, saying that she would of course pay the money back that they had borrowed. Alan said that there was no need, to take it as a gift, but she wouldn't accept this. She was a very attractive woman in her late thirties, but other than to say that she had been married, she did not go into any further detail. Alan again was left with the impression that she was not being totally open.

Later after they had eaten she asked whether she might have a private word with Alan. They went to his study. She again thanked him profusely for his kindness and then explained that she was married to a Monsieur de Vivier. He was an extremely wealthy wine grower, one of the largest in the Bordeaux region. They lived in Bordeaux and within a year or two of them being married he had started hitting her, and whilst she had put up with it when her daughter Avril was born, she discovered that he had also hit Avril. She immediately decided to leave him and knowing that he would not agree to this departed early one morning when he was out for a couple of days working away. She had packed a simple suitcase and just left with her daughter. She had managed to board a small cargo vessel without being seen and then hidden in the lifeboat. The vessel was sailing to Ireland where they hoped to find another boat and sail to America.

During the crossing to Ireland a severe storm blew up and the ship was wrecked. The lifeboat was washed overboard with them in it, and they were eventually able after two days at sea to spot a small island. They left the boat and swam to the island – Alan's island. She didn't want to go back to France, as she didn't want her husband to know that she was alive. He would only come and take them back to Bordeaux, which she definitely didn't want for either herself or for Avril. At this point she started to tell Alan a little about the life on island. She said, "You have been so kind and wonderful to us and I have stolen from you, I have cheated on you, I am very sorry." Alan didn't understand what she was talking about until she opened her bag and produced a feast of jewels, diamond rings and necklaces.

"Those are not mine," said Alan, "I have never seen those before." She said, "We found them on the island in the cave."
"Well then you must keep them," said Alan. "I don't need them, but perhaps we should go back and have a look at the cave and see whether there is anything else there." And so this was agreed upon.

Chantal had obviously got a weight off her mind and she started to relax. She was indeed a good looking woman and Alan was very impressed. She spoke good English and seemed to be well educated. Edward took them back to their cottage that night after Alan had said he would see them in a day or two and perhaps make arrangements to return to the island.

CHAPTER 27

After dinner that night, Edward mentioned to Alan that both the girls and boys would like to see him, and so a little later he invited them into his study. They were really quite excited and brought with them a large framed map of *Murray Island*. They had gone to a great deal of trouble and presented it to him. Alan studied the map. The outline of the island was really very well done indeed, and they had marked all the contours culminating in the highest point on the island which was middle to north of the island, just over 2,000ft high. The girls had noted on the map all the sightings they had made – there were Macaws or parrots quite widely spread across the island and wild pigs (they thought pigs rather than wild boar). The biggest surprise that had nearly scared them out of their wits was a whole small area on the island which had been virtually taken over by what appeared to be turkeys. They had also put onto the map all the fauna, various exotic trees, and it was really a work of art.

Alan was absolutely delighted and thanked them most profusely for it. He found a place to hang it in his library where they could refer to it as required. The anthropologist still had to make out his report and Alan was looking forward to that. Alan asked if they would you like to go to the island again this weekend if the weather was fine, and of course they wanted to go. Alan said he would have a word with Edward and see what could be arranged.

The following day Gerald suggested to Alan that he could take over *Endeavour* and have it as his own personal yacht. Perhaps it could be used for demonstration purposes. So that weekend, for the very first time they went to the island on *Endeavour*. The whole household went and were dropped off in the bay and then Alan, Edward, William Stones (the lad from the garden) and Chantal and Avril all sailed back out of the bay and round the island, trying to find the small sandy cove where Chantal and Avril had made land after the shipwreck. It took a considerable time, but eventually it was Avril who said, "That's it, that's the one, definitely!" So they moored up, got out the tender and motored ashore.

The beach was very narrow, only about 5 yards before the rock face rose vertically to 20ft or more, and there appeared to be no way of getting onto the island. Avril ran up the beach – she knew exactly where she was going – jumped on a rock and disappeared into the face of the cliff. Chantal explained that Avril had come down many times and gone swimming in the sea, so she knew her way very well. They all followed. About two metres above the height of the sand they espied a very narrow entrance into the rock. They each climbed and crept through and inside a huge cavern opened up.

Edward had come prepared and had taken a small generator and three trailing lights, which were passed through into the cavern, so soon the whole cavern was lit up. It really was huge. They could have got the whole of *Endeavour* in there. It was very high, and of course Chantal and Avril had never seen it lit up and so it was quite strange to them. They moved across to one side of the cavern and began feeling with their fingers where they had previously found jewels. Very soon there was an exclamation that there were more – a lot more. Digging around gently with the spade they had brought with them, they found two large caskets. Both were strongly bolted, but they felt sure that each one was full of treasure. They searched the rest of the cavern and found another huge metal box which when they were able to undo, and jewels of all types fell out. They search around a bit more and were unable to find anything else.

Chantal asked if they would like to see where they had lived for the last five years. So they all trouped up to the end of the cavern which gradually went upwards. They could see that daylight was coming through from the end of the cavern and a sloping floor lead them straight to an entrance. They spilled out onto the island itself. Glorious sunshine in contrast to the darkness of the cavern. Their camp was really well made. They had used trunks and branches of the trees and provided quite a large covered area where Chantal explained they prepared their food and where they also slept. It was really a very enterprising camp and Alan was impressed.

They went back down into the cavern, dragged the trunks towards the entrance onto the beach with great difficulty, all of them struggling. Each one was loaded one at a time onto the dinghy, taken out to *Endeavour* and using the pulley system on *Endeavour* brought on board. They sailed back into the bay and were greeted by the rest of the household. The BBQ was virtually ready and they discovered that they were very hungry indeed.

The following week Alan invited the British Museum to examine his find. Toward the end of the week two people came from the museum. They carefully and very delicately tried to open the two chests that were still sealed up and eventually had to resort to a hammer and chisel. Once inside they were packed with diamonds, all sorts of precious stones, gold, silver – it was just too much to imagine. It all spewed out over the library floor. The men from the museum wanted to catalogue it and photograph it, and to see where it was found. It was agreed that Alan and Edward would take them to the island the following day, weather permitting. Alan felt that Chantal and Avril should also be invited to come along, since it was really their find.

Two more people, ladies from the museum turned up the following day, one a photographer. They all sailed to the island. Avril of course lead the way into the cavern. The people from the museum were quite astonished. It was obviously a storage place for the pirates of years gone by – in fact they felt that with the chests, being found in different parts of the cave meant that more than one pirate had used the cave as his 'safe deposit'. Edward had again taken the generator and lighting. They spent some time photographing the entrance and the cave itself. They were really fascinated by it.

Back in the library they spent the next seven days cataloguing and photographing every item of this immense treasure trove. Their estimated value was in excess of billions, and nothing like it had been found previously.

The big problem now of course was security. Quite a lot of people knew about the find and it would not be long before something got out. The museum people said that they would gladly take it and store it. Alan agreed that the only thing to do was to put it up for sale. He decided, however, that every member of the household, including Chantal and Avril, should all choose a piece they would like to keep. So each in turn was invited in to the library and allowed to take away a piece of jewellery. Alan accepted a signature against the catalogue items and kept the photographs, and the people from the museum took the treasure away. It had been a hugely exciting and extremely profitable time.

Alan had decided that he would have an investigator look into the whereabouts of Chantal's husband, Monsieur de Vivier. He sent the private eye that he had previously used across to Bordeaux with strict instructions that he must not reveal who he was or who he was trying to investigate. There must be no connection, no feedback.

Within a couple of days he had rung Alan and said that, as far as he could discover, Monsieur de Vivier had been an extremely wealthy, well established wine producer, whose great hobby was power boat racing. He had been killed in a powerboat accident six months ago. There was a big mystery that his wife had disappeared five years previously and nobody knew where she was or whether she was still alive. His estate, which was huge, was being held for a further period under French law.

Alan went down to see Chantal that evening. He made sure that Avril could not overhear them and he told Chantal that he had some very important news. First of all he apologised for sending out a private investigator without her knowledge and said he had come up with some interesting information. "It appears your husband was killed six months ago in a powerboat accident. His estate is in limbo because they are unable to trace his wife, yourself. I think you ought to consider taking some action to recover the monies on the estate, if not for yourself, then for Avril." Alan indicated that he was willing to go with Chantal to Bordeaux, but first they should wait for the return of the private investigator who would give them both a first-hand report. Chantal really couldn't take it all in.

The private investigator turned up two days later. He had the full written report of course for Alan, but Alan invited him together with Chantal for dinner. He explained exactly what he had done. He had had very little difficulty locating where the de Viviers lived and who they were. He was an extremely well known and prominent person in Bordeaux, and he quickly established that Monsieur de Vivier had been killed in a disastrous accident involving two powerboats that were racing. The investigator had gone on to establish the value of the estate and confirmed that it was held in chancery which would be for a further 18 months under French law. The lawyers had been searching extensively for his wife, Chantal de Vivier, and daughter Avril, but no trace had been found of them.

Alan and Chantal had agreed before the meeting not to disclose who she was. Alan had made some excuse about trying to buy some equipment that was owned by the de Viviers.

Chantal said that of course she must go to Bordeaux, but would need to get leave of absence from the school. Eventually two weeks later Alan and Chantal set out for Bordeaux. Alan flew them in his aeroplane, and on reaching Bordeaux Chantal immediately went to see her own lawyers. They were astonished and surprised, as they had spent a considerable amount of time and money trying to find her, but she had just totally disappeared. In fact they had involved the Gendarmerie, because the circumstances had seemed quite suspicious. It took over a week to clear up all the facts and affirm them for the legal process, so Chantal took the opportunity to introduce Alan to some of her friends. They were all of course delighted that she had returned and everything appeared alright. They asked after Avril and she assured them that the girl was well and fit. They all seemed delighted that she was back. They had been extremely worried and unable to do anything as she had just disappeared.

Chantal took Alan to her house, a huge Chateau. The house had been closed up and was a bit like a morgue, but you could tell that it had been a most magnificent place which just needed some 'TLC'. The solicitors had seen to the business side of the estate. The wine producing had continued as normal, and all the staff had been retained.

Chantal said she must now return to England and tell Avril all about it. This she did. The following week they both left to go back to Bordeaux permanently. They said goodbye to all the friends they had met in Eden Stanton and they both thanked Alan once again for his help and generosity, agreeing to keep in touch. Chantal said that Alan must of course come to Bordeaux any time he wished and stay with them.

Alan flew up to Sunderland to see his mother. She had a bit of cold, but was otherwise very well. He went round to see his sister, Alison and her family were all well. His mother agreed that she would break with tradition and spend Christmas with him at *Parklands* and Alison also agreed that they would all come down for the Christmas break. He telephoned his brother Charles, and again it was agreed that they would meet up at his house for Christmas. Gilly would not come back with him as he had wanted her too – she said that she was perfectly alright as she was, had lots of friends and people dropping in and was not at all unhappy with her life. So with that Alan flew back to *Parklands*.

Edward had been taking flying lessons for some time and now had his licence so he took the plane back to the small aerodrome, leaving it there. Alan had given considerable thought to what he was going to do with the money from the treasure trove. He decided that the first thing was to agree the best possible sale and to put the money into trust. It would be a charitable trust, and he was thinking in terms of building a hospital and possibly a school as the area badly needed both. His lawyers drew up the necessary papers to put the money into a charitable trust. He instructed the museum to dispose at the best possible price.

Production of the EHS units was proceeding at pace. The new factory was in full production and already ten machines had been delivered to the USA. Alistair had gone out with them, to instruct the Americans in how to use them.

The first stealth boat was also off the production line, and totally magnificent. The hull and super structure were all in a matt black, and even at dusk on the water you could hardly see it. It laid low in the water, but of course as the speed increased it rose out of the water. In tests it had done over 85 knots and was completely stable and extremely comfortable. The accommodation for the 30 marines all seated had hydraulic sprung seats, so any rough motion of the boat was taken out by the hydraulics – a clever system that Jim Caldwell had a major hand in developing.

Gerald and the production manager took Alan out for an extended night passage on the new boat and it performed fantastically. The speed and manoeuvrability and all the electronics functioned perfectly, and it was really everything that both Alistair and Alan had dreamed about. The production was proving relatively easy and the boats were starting to flow through the factory.

Alan suggested that they ought to carry out some tests on the stealth side. Initially perhaps this should be carried out on a cargo vessel, but he really wanted to try this out on an unsuspecting naval vessel. When they turned to go back to the shipyard they came across a small cargo vessel. Alistair operated the electronics and put the entire ship in darkness, only for about five seconds, but sufficient to ensure that Alan saw it worked. It was a very impressive demonstration. Back to the boatyard they went. Keeping the boat under wraps was important. Alan went away with two problems – firstly to try and initiate another test with a naval vessel, and secondly to invite his American friends for a demonstration.

It was 3.00 in the morning. Edward was knocking on Alan's door. "Sorry to disturb you, sir, an urgent phone call for you." It was Gerald. "Sorry to bother you, but some of the plans for the boat are missing. Everybody's up searching for them," he explained. "Where are you now?" Alan asked. "At the shipyard," said Gerald.

Alan arrived 20 minutes later. The office was full of all the senior staff. Someone explained that the plans for the stealth boat were missing. "Which plans exactly?" asked Alan. There were three drawings of the hull – not detailed, but just overall plans. They had a tight security system on all drawings and a minimum number were issued. Any drawing was booked out, signed for and had to be returned that same day. A drawing getting into the wrong hands could be disastrous. Alan went through what had happened step-by-step – they must have been stolen. He called his high-level contact at the police , to try and stop this news getting into the papers.

A Detective Sergeant arrived and went through the whole sequence of events. The chances of tracing the drawings were remote. There was nothing more that could be done, and everyone returned to their beds. Next morning, Alan called all the managers to a meeting. He explained about the missing drawings, and put one person in charge of reviewing all the existing security systems. This was of the utmost importance.

The following day the Chief Constable rang. "Alan," he explained, "we have discovered your lost drawings. A car was stopped for a motoring offense and an eagle-eyed officer spotted a roll of drawings on the flor of the vehicle. They are definitely yours – there are five drawings altogether." Alan thanked the police and called each of the managers who were involved – the emergency was over. It was a timely warning!

CHAPTER 28

Christmas 1997 was fast approaching. All of the staff at *Parklands* had independently said that they would prefer to stay there over the Christmas period, visiting their own families where appropriate just for the odd day. Alan invited Josh and his girlfriend Julia, and of course Molly and her daughter Barbara, to come for Christmas Day and spend the night. He also invited Gerald and Dr Jane and Jim Caldwell and Alistair.

It was going to be pretty busy Christmas, so Edward got all the staff together and between them they decided who was going to do what. A huge Christmas tree was bought for the hall and the decorations put up. Three days before Christmas Alan and Edward flew up to Sunderland. They picked up Gilly, Alan's mother, and drove out to the landing strip. His sister Alison, husband and two teenage children were waiting for them and were loaded into the plane and off they flew home to *Parklands*. Brother Charles drove down with his family the following day.

It was the first time that Gilly had ever been in an aeroplane. She thoroughly enjoyed the flight, which fortunately was a smooth one, and when they landed at *Parklands* everyone was impressed. The children were particularly taken with the deer. They went into the house and Edward took them each to their respective bedrooms. Charles and his family arrived the following day. They had had a good journey, albeit a long one, and the children were pleased to reach their destination.

The previous week Alan had spent almost two days shopping for Christmas presents. He had enlisted the help of his secretary Karen, who was excellent at these things, and between them they chose suitable presents for everybody. The Christmas tree was a delight and the girls, with occasional help from the lads, decorated it superbly – even Edward was pleased with what they had achieved. Alan had all his presents put under the tree and as the guests found their way about the house they also brought their presents down and placed them – there appeared to be hundreds of them!

Back at the shipyards and the scanner workshop Alan had given every employee a good Christmas bonus. All his companies had had an excellent year, so he was able in this way to thank them all for the part they had played.

Christmas Day arrived at *Parklands*. It was going to be quite a party. There was Gilly, his mother, sister Alison and her husband and the two children, brother Charles and his wife and their two children, Josh and Julia arrived bringing Molly and Barbara with them, George, his wife Betty the cook, three girls, Bridget, Jean and Jill, and the boys out of the garden, Gerard and William, Dr James, Jim Caldwell and Alister, not forgetting Suzanne, Bill, Catherine and Alan, and of course Edward – twenty-nine people in all. Mrs Hetherington was of course in charge of Christmas dinner. She was assisted by Bridget, Jean and Jill.

By eleven o'clock in the morning all were assembled. The children had each had a sack in their bedrooms, but their main presents were under the tree. They were desperately searching and looking to see what size of present they had got. Alan sat Gilly down near the Christmas tree with the eldest of his nieces and asked her to hand out the presents from under the tree. By two o'clock in the afternoon they had decimated all the presents. There was paper everywhere and Edward was busy tidying up.

The table had been laid in the hall. With the huge fire burning in the grate and the Christmas tree at one end – it was a lovely setting and Mrs Hetherington announced that dinner was served. They all sat down. Edward said 'grace' and they tucked in to a wonderful meal, the turkey of course being the crowning glory – in fact with such a large gathering, there were two turkeys, each stuffed with Betties' favourite stuffing. Alan carved one turkey and Edward the other, and as Alan carved the bird, an acorn fell out. Alan insisted that after dinner everyone had to go and plant the acorn in the front of the house. (Sure enough, a year later, a small fragile tree was growing, and today it is nearly 20ft high.)

The turkeys were followed by an enormous Christmas pudding which was carried in by Gerald and William when fully alight and burning. It was quite a sight. The food was excellent. Betty Hetherington had done a splendid job and at the end of the meal Alan made a short speech, thanking all of his staff for making the first Christmas at *Parklands* an event to remember. The girls organised some simple party games and after lunch they played these until it was time for a splendid cold tea of ham and chicken. Several of the guests had long since put their heads back and were snoring gently in their chairs. Alan decided that he needed some exercise and so had taken the children all wrapped up out to the garden. They visited the deer and went down to the lake. By the time the day had ended everyone was tired and happy. They had had a wonderful Christmas Day.

On Boxing Day most of the family went out to watch the local hunt, which they followed on foot for a little while, the children enjoying the horses and hounds and of course the huntsmen all dressed in pink. On the following days Alan took small parties of adults to visit his various activities – the shipyard, the farm, and they all began to realise that Alan was very much a captain of industry, a wealthy man who had totally changed his life around. They were of course delighted for him and kept teasing him as to when he would meet the girl of his dreams.

Eventually all his guests drifted back to their own homes with fond farewells, but Gilly asked whether she could stay a little longer – of course Alan was delighted and said she could stay as long as she wished. She said, "No, just another week please," but at the end of that week she said, "Perhaps could I stay another week?" So in the end it became the second week of February before Alan took her back home. She had had a lovely Christmas and holiday and said that perhaps she could come back in the summer. Of course Alan said she could come any time.

CHAPTER 29

Early in the New Year Alan contacted Bob Calendar and told him that they had produced a prototype of the stealth ship. About a week later Bob rang him and said that he had organised a group of about ten people from the US, including the Secretary of Defence, a number of other leading politicians and army personnel. Bob said, "I hope it's alright, but I have asked them to come a week on Thursday." Alan replied, "No problem, we'll set up a proper demonstration for you. But you must realise a real demonstration must take place at night and we could really do with an American Naval ship which we could 'attack'."

Bob responded that he would organise something. Gerald Birch worked hard on all the details. The appointed day arrived. It was the third week of February. Fortunately the weather was reasonable and around about four o'clock in the afternoon a party made their way down to the shipyard. The boat was ready for them. They were all taken aback by what they saw. It looked like a rather large whale. Access was by a side hatch and once inside they could see what was happening in the outside world through a series of monitors. Bob had also supplied ten marines who were, of course, sworn to secrecy. Gerald had set up a slave speed recorder which they could look at.

He boarded the ten marines and they started out, quickly moving up to a speed of 85 knots. The motion inside the boat was not difficult and nobody thank goodness was ill. Gerald had been communicating with Bob Calendar. They had informed the commanding officer of one the American cruisers visiting Great Britain that they would try and approach it, possibly cut out its light, and board the vessel leaving some sign that they had boarded. The commanding officer somewhat hesitantly agreed that he would keep this information under his hat and would not take any precautions that he would not normally take and see what happened.

They slowed down on approach, knowing that at these speeds, about 15-20 knots, they were virtually invisible to the radar systems. They came alongside the cruiser and remotely turned off all its lights and navigation equipment and killed their engines. From the inside of the stealth ship they were able to observe the apparent panic on board through infra-red camera. The marines, all ten of them, boarded the ship and left a British Union Jack in a prominent place over one of the guns. They then returned, settled back into the stealth and moved away from the cruiser. They released the cruiser from its misery, turning its lights and engines back on, set the course back for home.

All the visitors were totally impressed. They had never seen or even thought that such a thing could happen. By now back at the shipyard it was midnight, and Alan suggested that they all took to their beds and reconvene for breakfast at his house at nine o'clock the next morning. This duly happened. Having slept on the presentation, the Secretary of Defence announced that he was totally sold on the system and would be reporting back to his committee with a very positive attitude.

They all thanked Alan and Gerald and his crew for a very efficient and convincing demonstration. Bob Calendar said that he had contacted the commanding officer of the cruiser and he was totally astounded how anything like this could have occurred to his ship. He really found it very hard to believe that it was reported to him that a British Union Jack had been draped and fastened over one of the guns. He apologised profusely to Bob, who said, "Don't worry we are going to have it on our side." The whole presentation had been a total and outstanding success. Bob Calendar said that he would put in a requisition for 200 boats as he had earlier promised.

CHAPTER 30

Over the next few weeks, Alan and Gerald put their heads together. Alan suggested that they went up to Sunderland and look over the old Sunderland shipbuilder's yards, which they did. They spent three or four days up there, looking over the shipyards themselves and the offices. Gerald said, "If we moved our production up here, we would certainly be able to do all the fibre glass moulding. We would be able to manoeuvre and with a fair degree of security." Alan agreed.

The owners of the yard were the British Government. The yards had lain empty since 1983. Alan and Gerald worked out staffing level requirements and rough capital costings on various production numbers and went armed with all this information to the Ministry, asking for a considerable Government Grant towards restoring a part of the Sunderland shipyards. He also approached the British Admiralty and told them of the success he had had with the Americans. Eventually they came back to see him for a demonstration.

Then an order came that totally astounded Alan, for 5,000 boats from the Secretary of Defence in the States. The boats were to be used for several different applications – as attack boats, in various theatres of war, and also to be used extensively in conjunction with the scanner that was already on order with Alan for the fight against illegal immigration and particularly drugs.

Armed with these orders, Alan flew up to London and met up again with the Ministry owning the Sunderland shipyard. They agreed peppercorn rent for the yards and grant aid of £2.5 million to put parts of the yard back into some resemblance of order. The Americans agreed an initial delivery rate of 1,000 ships per annum, but the first year to be an 18 month year. The utmost secrecy was to be retained.

It was back to the drawing board again; organise staffing, develop the yard and the whole organisation from the top down. The production manager of Cornish Shipbuilders decided that he really preferred to stay in charge of the yacht building side of the business, as this was his forte, so he was to stay in Cornwall. A new production director and managing director of the new company which was to be called Cornish Ships Ltd needed to be found to operate from Sunderland. Apart from the top official, they needed management and technical expertise on the fibreglass build side. They needed top class electronics management, and finally fitting out, launching and organising. In addition to all of that, the shipyard itself had to be re-hashed – buildings pulled down and new sheds organised to take much smaller boats than they had previously been designed for. Alan had agreed with the American administration that they were to pay a deposit of ten per cent. Since the ships were costing about £2 million each the total order was £10 billion, so a deposit of £1 billion was paid over.

While all this energy was being expended on the new stealth vessel, the first 100 scanner units had been delivered to the States. Both Alistair and Jim Caldwell spent nearly four weeks in the States at the beginning of the year, instructing the first 20 or so operators how the equipment should be used and how it all worked. Within a few months the equipment was installed and operating. It worked absolutely perfectly. All those involved were really excited at how the equipment could solve their illegal immigration and more particularly the drugs smuggling. It was already starting to pay off. The success of this project had undoubtedly encouraged the powers-that-be in the States to move forward with their order for the stealth ship.

Alan and Gerald moved up to Sunderland on a semi-permanent basis. The idea was that they would spend about four weeks organising everything and getting the staff in place, and then return to their offices at Eden Stanton. Things however proved a lot more difficult and everything happened a lot more slowly. Alan asked Josh to join them to help with the refurbishment of the yard and offices in Sunderland. It was six months before they were able to return to Eden Stanton on a permanent basis. The people in Sunderland were delighted that someone had had the initiative to open up their shipyards again, albeit on a much smaller scale than previously. By the end of September, 2,000 people had been recruited and production was getting underway.

The rest of the year past quickly and Christmas 1998 again was held at *Parklands*. Gilly was again in high spirits, despite her age, and was the heart and soul of the party. She stayed on again until well into February, thoroughly enjoying the help and service she got from all the staff. 1999 opened up what was to become a very busy year. In the course of the previous year they had supplied five yachts and the order level had increased. They intended to build a further ten yachts in 1999. The scanner was in full production, and so also were the stealth ships. Alan had hardly seen the island the previous year. The children of course made full use of it, and also the remaining house staff had gone out there at various times. Alan resolved that this year he would make time to enjoy himself a little.

The follow up orders for the scanner had come in and there were over 500 on order from the States. Alan felt it was time to try and interest the British Government in the project. It was nearly three years since he had first contacted them and had no response, but now with the orders from the USA coming in, and the stealth ship project, he was starting to get known in government circles. He wrote to the Prime Minister extolling the virtues of the scanners, explaining how successful they were being in America. He also again pointed out that all this information was very secret and should be treated as such.

He had a reply within seven days from the Prime Minister asking him to visit 10 Downing Street and make a short presentation to himself, the Home Secretary and the Minister of Defence. Alan rang immediately and made an appointment for the following week. At the meeting Alan described the system and explained how the Americans were using it to great advantage. He also mentioned that the development of the stealth ship was interconnected with this system, and the success of the scanner had been largely responsible for the speed at which it had been accepted and ordered by the Americans. He went on to say that the only real way for the British Government to evaluate either of these systems was to have a full demonstration which would take a day and a night. He suggested the Prime Minister, Home Secretary and Minister of Defence, and perhaps one or two other cabinet ministers together with technical people, should attend this demonstration. He also mentioned that because of the American orders and other interest from around the world they were unlikely to be able to make any deliveries in the next 18 months or so. The PM agreed and said he would re-contact Alan in the next few weeks.

A few weeks later a demonstration visit had been organised. They went through exactly the same procedure as they had done with the Americans and took a party of fifteen people out on one of the stealth ships. They were able to get in close to a British frigate that was coming up the Channel at the time. Alan moved in, cut off the engine and the lights, totally unseen. It was a very impressive demonstration. They had arrived in time for lunch and it was after 1.00 am when Alan said goodbye them. They were all pretty tired by this time and promised to be in touch. It was not until the end of 1999 that he received an enquiry from the MOD for the cost of 20 scanners and 20 stealth ships.

CHAPTER 31

Early in 1999 Lord Copperfield, the Lord of the Manor passed away. He was only 79 years old, but had been in poor health for a number of years. He had no heir and his death left a large vacuum over the estate and the three farms that made up his heritage. Alan decided to buy all three farms and eventually the National Trust took over the house and gardens. It was an additional 2,500 acres, making his total farmland well over 3,000 acres in size.

The time had come to set future policy for his farming exploits. Alan was very keen on organic farming – he had been on the fringe of this for the last three years and had taken expert advice. He now took on one of the leading people in organic farming, Jim Bird, who was only 35 years of age and already recognised as very much a technical leader in organic farming. Alan told him of his plans to increase his acreage to 250,000 acres over perhaps a period of the next five years. This of course was private information, as he did not wish farm prices to go against him. Alan and Jim laid out the full principles over the next three or four months. This included the centralisation control of how every field should be planted, computerisation of the exact background to every field, its yield, etc. The whole basis of farming under an organic system.

Jim visited the four farms that were now under Alan's authority. Three of the farmers agreed to stay on and work the new system, one left saying that it would not work. They amalgamated the three farms from the Copperfield Estate and moved it into two. In the course of his various trips to London and the dinners that he had attended, he had met up with His Royal Highness, the Prince of Wales. They had talked at some length about his organic farming desires. He wrote to the Prince and invited him to *Parklands* to meet up with Jim Bird, and perhaps also to have dinner one evening with the American Generals.

Much to his amazement, he had a response almost immediately from His Royal Highness accepting, explaining that they (meaning himself and the Duchess of Cornwall) would be available to spend the weekend with him in four weeks time. He was to arrive early evening on the Friday and spend Saturday and Sunday with him, leaving early on the Monday morning. Alan was delighted and informed his staff, telling them of course that this information was not to be disclosed. Mrs Hetherington jumping up and down as to what manner of food she should produce! Alan invited Bob Calendar and his wife, Jasmine and Ian McKenzie and his wife, Veronica and made sure that his daughter Suzanne was available for the weekend.

CHAPTER 32

The visit was to take place during June. Prior to inviting Prince Charles, Alan had received an invitation from the Queen to receive a Knighthood which he had accepted with alacrity. He was able to attend the Knighthood ceremony early in June, thus when he received the Prince of Wales and Duchess of Cornwall and their entourage, together with all his other friends, he was now Sir Alan Brown. Congratulations came from all, and the people in the village were delighted, as were the council and his growing friends in Sunderland.

Over the weekend when the Prince arrived they spent considerable time discussing organic farming. The Prince was taken to Alan's shipyard and fell in love with the yachts and decided that he would place an order for one. On the Sunday, the whole party, together with the Americans went out on three vessels to the island where they had a celebratory BBQ. It was a wonderful weekend and the weather was spectacular. The Prince of Wales and Duchess of Cornwall thanked him for such a relaxing and comfortable weekend which they had enjoyed. They promised they would reciprocate and asked him to invite them back again. Sir Alan of course agreed.

The year passed with the first deliveries of the stealth ship being made culminating in over 1,000 orders by the end of the year. Christmas 1999 with all the family was held at *Parklands*. The New Year, the Year 2000 – the Millennium, was celebrated in style. Gilly stayed until well into February, and towards the end of February Alan was invited to give a lecture at The Royal Horticultural Society in London on organic farming. With persuasion from Jim Bird he accepted and spent a considerable time preparing his lecture. He was astonished by the enthusiasm with which his lecture announcement was received.

On the appointed day he made good measure of himself. The press were extremely persistent and it was decided to hold a separate press conference at the end of the lecture. There was a young lady, one of the press reporters, who stood out from the crowd in Alan's eyes, but she found great difficulty in getting a question to him. She kept being 'bullied' by the rest of the reporting fraternity. Alan asked his agent who she was and sent round a note asking her to join him after the conference. He gave her nearly three-quarter-of-an-hour interview and she was absolutely delighted. She had researched Alan extensively and had prepared an excellent paper of well worthwhile questions. She was indeed an extremely well-qualified young lady, with a first in English Literature at Oxford and also in Philosophy. At the end of the interview he made his mind up that he would ask her to write his biography. He liked the idea of creating a biography principally for his children. He had a reached an age where he would love to have known what his father and grandfathers had done, but there was no one that he really could talk to.

Sarah West was delighted to be invited to do Alan's biography. She had already researched his background and had discovered that he was an interesting person. She was also finding it difficult to earn a good living as a freelance reporter – she loved writing but somehow found it difficult to get involved. She felt this biography would really set her up, so she was determined to make a first-class job of it. She came down to *Parklands* and after a week or so moved into rented accommodation in the village, which gave her the independence she needed. Initially she had several fairly long meetings with Sir Alan, discussing the whole of his background, contacts and general information. She asked Sir Alan whether she could have a two-hour meeting twice a week, with some flexibility.

Bill, Alan's son, had been at university now for two years. He was at Bath doing a degree in architecture, which he had wanted to do for a considerable time. Alan was delighted and encouraged him, and Bill was enjoying university, the lifestyle and the freedom.

Suzanne, now 26 had had four years in industrial employment after university. She was a manufacturing engineer. Alan had a word with Gerald Birch who said "We can definitely use as many engineers as we can get hold of, but of course it will be based in Sunderland."

After thinking quite carefully through the implications Alan had a word with Suzanne. "How would you like to join the company?" he asked.
"Oh yes I would," she replied.
"The problem is this would be in Sunderland."
"Ok, no problem. How about Catherine – she is a servo mechanism engineer and she is extremely well thought of. Could you use her?"
Alan said he would see what Gerald and the other engineers had to say, but he thought they definitely could. Then Suzanne dropped the bombshell.
"By the way Dad, I've got a serious boyfriend. Can I bring him down to *Parklands* next weekend?"
"Of course you can," said Alan. He was quite pleased that she was now thinking about settling down.

The boyfriend turned up the following weekend. His name was Gareth Hughes and he seemed a decent sort of fellow. He was an engineer as well, about the same age as Suzanne, and worked for the same company. Alan got on with him well, so he left things to develop. Both Suzanne and Catherine joined Cornwall Shipbuilders. Most of the time they were stationed at Sunderland where they also lived.

CHAPTER 33

Everything seemed to be working extremely well. The stealth boats were well on target as were the scanners, and they had sold the ten yachts which they had hoped to this year. Alan was feeling that he would like to take a holiday. He had no ideas of where or what to do, but just felt like getting away for a change. Just as he was thinking this a letter arrived. It was from Chantal de Vivier in Bordeaux. She had at long last settled the estate of her husband, had taken on new staff for the Chateau and was well entrenched. "Come and have a holiday with us," she said. "Avril would love to see you again and so would I." The invitation arrived at just the right moment and Alan decided to take it up. He would drive to Bordeaux because he would enjoy the journey. He was thinking whether to take anyone with him, but thought not and decided to go away for up to four weeks. This would also give Edward and the staff at *Parklands* a chance to have a holiday and a break. He wrote straight back to Chantal and in his letter said, "I hope you can put up with me. I am arriving next week."

Edward was astonished as Alan had not gone on holiday before and so agreed as both he and the rest of the staff would enjoy a break. The following week Alan drove to Bordeaux. He took two days over the trip. He called in and had a night in Paris and then stopped again in the Dordogne. He had not be there for many years and had made good friends in the past, so he called in on his acquaintances and they were delighted to see him and insisted that he stayed the night. It wasn't until Thursday that he arrived in Bordeaux.

Chantal was delighted to see him and immediately made him very welcome and he had the most wonderful room in the Chateau. She was obviously an extremely wealthy woman now. Avril arrived home from school later in the afternoon and was thrilled to see Alan. She flung her arms around him and gave him a big kiss.

After dinner that night Chantal and Alan sat down with their coffees. "You know," she said, "being wealthy like I am has its drawbacks, I am only a young woman and if the opportunity arose I would like to get married again to the right fellow. Finding the right person in my position is extremely difficult."
Alan agreed with her, "I don't think I would rush things you know. Perhaps the answer would be to go on an extended holiday or cruise and maybe you would meet someone there! But I don't think you can set out and look for the right person, it's just got to happen."
Chantal agreed with him.

In bed that night Alan went over the conversation and wondered whether in fact Chantal was sort of proposing to him. Certainly she was very attractive, well educated and now an extremely wealthy woman, but Alan was not interested at all, not in that way anyway.

That weekend Chantal invited some friends round and they had a wonderful dinner party on the Saturday night. Everyone spoke English because Alan's French was really very poor. In the days that followed he and Chantal drove around the Bordeaux region, right down to the beaches at Piladoon where they had a lovely time. The weather was gorgeous – a bit too hot for Alan though, but it was very different and very relaxing and he enjoyed every moment of it.

Coming back to the Chateaux each evening they had the most wonderful food. Chantal's cook was really magic and Alan felt very relaxed and very comfortable. Chantal's friend, whom he had met at the dinner party, invited them both out for a week's cruise on his yacht and Alan jumped at the chance. He enjoyed sailing and this was an opportunity to see how another boat performed.

It was a large yacht, 80ft in length, beautifully appointed and he had his own cabin. There were six people on the boat and they sailed down the French coast to Biarritz, round the corner to Portugal and down to Porto and then on to Lisbon. The weather seemed set. They sailed on again down the bottom of Portugal to Cadiz visiting Gibraltar – it was a fantastic trip. They had taken nearly twelve days to sail down and now everyone felt that they needed to get back. Alan was all for sailing, but the pressure was on other people so they decided to leave the boat in Cadiz and fly back to Bordeaux.

He had a few more days with Chantal and Avril and then bade his farewells, thanking them for such a wonderful holiday. He drove up the east side of France to Lyon and then through the Champagne area of France, and finally to England. He drove right across the south of England and was back home at *Parklands*. He had been away for over four weeks, but was pleased to be back home again and everybody seemed happy to have him back home.

CHAPTER 34

Alan had not met up with Jim Bird for quite a number of months so he decided they ought to have a meeting. The following week Jim came along with a full presentation. He had really done his homework taking the concept for the very large area farms, particularly in southern Cornwall, to go organic. He had produced a synopsis of every single farm in the area, over 300 of them. The average acreage was just over 300 – some were quite small, but others large. There was no doubt that farming in the area was marginally profitable if run well, and so a lot of farmers were keen to dispose of their farms and sell up as they had had enough. Jim had created a programme of farm takeovers showing the ones that were possible, the majority, and those 'hard nuts' that would not sell. In his synopsis he had suggested a minimum sized farm should be 600-700 acres. Farms would be amalgamated, and he had again drawn up a plan of how this could happen. He had then drawn out a programme of gradual acquisition over a period of 10 years and a progressive change-over to organic cropping and breeding.

Turning to Alan's existing farms, the two original and the three that had come his way from the Copperfield Estates, he confirmed that the amalgamation to two farms was the right way to go. He had drawn up a plan of these farms and again a changeover to organic. Jim had done an excellent detailed and comprehensive plan. He had attempted to put some figures of costs towards the acquisition and development. The big problem was to make the enterprise profitable. There was a great deal of room for thought and Alan asked Jim if he could put down some projected production costs and compare that to existing prices.

The following week Alan asked Josh to come and see him. He showed him the programme that Jim had created for the acquisition of approximately 300 farms and the development of the existing farms. He asked Josh to consider whether it was feasible and practical to go along with their re-design and development programme of converting disused farms and buildings into holiday homes and into houses for sale. Was the business profitable? Would there be sufficient demand over the next ten years? Alan also asked Josh for his overall opinion.

Alan's idea had been to develop his own chain of supermarkets selling produce from the farms at up to 50% more than the existing farmers were getting. This would mean a higher price in the supermarkets, but by cutting out any middlemen there would be some price saving. Alan needed help with the whole concept of farming and distributing organic foodstuffs in order that the next phase of the development would be profitable. He called in Andrew McBride, his internal accountant, who was well practiced in farming affairs. They had a good discussion and Andrew said that he would work on the project and see what he could come up with. He also contacted Jeremy Knight and asked whether he would help out and be involved with the project. He recommended a colleague of his and suggested that the three of them meet up in the near future. Alan also decided to consult ADAS, the Agricultural Society Advisory Service, who were based in the Midlands. Their consultant had been involved in various large cell projects of organic foodstuffs and cattle rearing.

CHAPTER 35

It was mid-August and the weather was really gorgeous – very warm and lots of sun. Alan was determined to go out to the island and spend some time there, so he sailed across on his own and went in to meet Amani and Kizzy. They were of course delighted to see him and both the boys were there on their breaks from university. Alan had never really seen much of the island and he persuaded George and the two boys to take him on a trip around the island for a couple of days or so. It was a fantastic experience. They reached the highest hill in the island, and the views were stunning in all directions. George carried out a few repairs to his communication aerials which had withstood the battering of all the weather there. Then they returned to the bay.

Alan was quite exhausted, but so thoroughly enjoyed the adventure. He relaxed for the next couple of days and on the Saturday the whole of the entourage from *Parklands* joined them. It really was the most wonderful place to crash out. It was no wonder he thought that Amani and Kizzy had wanted to stay on the island and not re-join civilisation. The boys of course were finding their feet on the mainland. They had made good friends, a few of whom had come to the island from time to time, but the boys were beginning to yearn for more of a 'life'.

Back home Alan decided to open their first farmers' supermarket, a small one in Bristol, just to test the water and see what prices he could get for the food that he was already growing on the farms. This farming business was going to take time – it was not going to have a fast track like his other businesses, but for the moment he was persisting with it.

Christmas again was drawing nigh and everyone so enjoyed the last year or so at *Parklands* they all wanted to come there again. Of course Alan was pleased. Gilly asked if it was possible for her to come down a bit early, say in November, perhaps to help with the Christmas preparations. She would love to do that, to have something to do. Alan of course agreed and again went up for Gilly, bringing her down to *Parklands*. This time however, he went by road – it was a change for Gilly and Alan was able to get around the north east a little bit and of course visited everyone there. They were all delighted to see him. They were now employing nearly 4,000 people and it was starting to make a real impression on the town. Alan spent ten days there visiting every part of the plant, talking to as many as he could.

He stayed with Gilly, who was pleased to see him and quite honestly to have someone to look after. She needed something to do, an object in life, and was really quite active and had all her faculties. Alison came over one day with the children and Alan was able to spend a bit of time talking to Alison regarding the farming of organic foodstuffs. Whilst her main training was household pets, she had studied both cattle and sheep farming in depth. She said she would read up on the whole subject and write him a report and bring it to him at Christmas. They were all looking forward to Christmas at *Parklands* and eventually Alan and Gilly drove back down south.

It was now towards the end of November and Christmas preparations were well in hand. Alan had a word with Mrs Hetherington and asked her if she would mind trying to find something for Gilly to do, explaining to her that he thought that she needed something to keep her occupied. She was capable of doing some cooking and he felt that his mother would really enjoy that. Mrs Hetherington said she would be delighted to involve her with the Christmas preparations and would enjoy having her company.

Alan told his mother that Mrs Hetherington would be pleased to have her assistance in the kitchen and Gilly was really quite pleased.

The Christmas tree was erected and the girls decorated it – it always looked splendid. Alan spent an entire day shopping with Karen's assistance. He had such a lot of presents to buy and Karen was such a whizz at this sort of thing, he didn't know what he would do without her.

A few days before Christmas Alison arrived. As good as her word she gave Alan her findings from a veterinary point of view of the organic foodstuffs. Her children were delighted to spend Christmas at *Parklands*, as was her husband. Charles arrived with his wife and children, again all excited waiting for Christmas Day.

Christmas Day duly arrived and Alan's favourite time was when Gilly sat next to the tree with the children handing out presents from under the tree. She handed them out one at a time to everyone present. Of course each present had to be opened before the next one was given out. It took ages and ages, and at the end of it there was a mountain of wrapping paper which Edward had done his best to keep under control.

Mrs Hetherington announced dinner was ready. A large table had been set in the hall and a wonderful feast awaited them. They all took their time over eating the magnificent meal. The Christmas pudding was especially scrumptious. Mrs Hetherington said she had made it from memory from an old recipe that her mother used to use. Afterwards they sat in the lounge, turned on the television and watched the Queen's speech, as they did every year. Even the children sat quietly after Alan said it would only last ten minutes and they must listen to every word she said! Afterwards they played silly games and had a wonderful time. They went out in the garden for a little with the dogs and some of the more energetic ones went for quite a long walk, but eventually they all drifted back. Sandwiches and a cup of tea were brought out, and despite protests that they couldn't eat any more, they all did. The Christmas cake was also a big success. Eventually the day wound to a close and everybody, tired went off to bed.

On Boxing Day Alan and a few others went off riding to meet up with the hunt. It was a Pony Club affair usually on Boxing Day, and there was a big turnout. Nobody really bothered whether they caught a fox or not, it was just a jolly good ride across the fields and the hounds thoroughly enjoyed it. Gradually, over the next few days, everybody departed with promises to come again next year. Gilly did as she had now been accustomed to, and said she would like to stay at least until February, which of course she did.

The following week it was the New Year – the Millennium. They had organised in the villages one great get-together at Eden Stanton. They had a fireworks display from the boats in the harbour, which was spectacular, and a sort of Cornish Pasty was served hot in the village hall – it really was a night to remember, Alan thoroughly enjoyed himself.

Almost immediately into the New Year Gerald showed Alan the prototype that he had been working on. It was a scanner put into a small suitcase, as far as Alan could see. The idea was that it was placed stationary in a prominent position. Vehicles were driven past it at a speed not exceeding 15mph, and with the device they were able to scan the whole of the vehicle from front to back, side to side, and immediately register if there were any drugs or human beings in the vehicle. It was a major breakthrough and a few weeks later, towards the end of March, Alan and Gerald took it to Customs House in London. They had prearranged a test where one or two vehicles carrying small amounts of drugs and another one carrying people interspersed with the normal traffic. The equipment worked splendidly. It picked out every vehicle with the drugs and immediately picked out the one carrying people. There was no doubt about it – the product was going to be a huge success.

The next morning Alan was at home having his weekly meeting with Sarah West, the young lady who was writing his biography. He met her at the door of his study. "Is this book not finished yet?"

"Yes," replied Sarah "it has been completed for several weeks now, I have asked two friends to read it through, which they have done with corrections, and I also showed it to my friend who is a publisher. He said he wanted to publish the book and would put in an advance of £150,000"

Alan replied, "That's wonderful, we must have a celebration!"

CHAPTER 36

My name is Sarah West and I was engaged to write Sir Alan Brown's biography. He said when he took me on that he thought it would take about a year, and a year to the day it was finished with the words, "That's wonderful! We must have a celebration!"

Throughout the year Sir Alan had not seemed that interested in the book. He was very busy with other things and I am afraid I was a bit of a nuisance really. However, let me start from the beginning.

I was christened Sarah Thurston West and born on 10th June 1964. My father was an important lawyer – he had a partnership, his own company West, West and partners Solicitors. My mother was also a solicitor who worked for someone else in our town, Great Malvern. I was an only child and after the first six months of my life a nanny was employed to look after me. Her name was Jean. I really had an idyllic life. War had ended and things were getting back to normal and my family were obviously comfortably off. We lived in a lovely part of the world, tucked into the elbow of the Malvern Hills. After going to prep school I eventually went to Malvern College where I enjoyed everything. The sports were absolutely fabulous – running, gymnastics, netball, hockey, tennis and squash – but the sports were all secondary to my studies. I just enjoyed classroom work. I did exceptionally well in my GCSEs and 'A'-Levels and eventually went up to Oxford to read English and Philosophy.

My parents dearly wished that I would join them and become a lawyer, but it was not what I wanted. I wanted journalism. After a few false starts I landed a small job with a local paper and starting at the bottom I thought I would work my way up. Of course I had one or two boyfriends, but nothing serious, and as the years went by I really failed to get a worthwhile job in journalism, and failed also to find a husband. I began to feel that life was going to pass me by. Then at the age of nearly 36, I attended this lecture by Sir Alan Brown. I had spent considerable time researching his background and intended to put together a good story. I was working freelance and was hoping I would get a worthwhile sum. Then of course Sir Alan offered me the job. I did complete the write up on Sir Alan and got paid quite handsomely for it, but I was glad to get away from journalism – it obviously was not my forté. I thought having written one or two minor books in the past that this was my big opportunity.

Sir Alan had asked me to come and see him in his room after the lecture. He explained that he had noticed that I was having difficulty in getting any questions in so made himself available for me to ask him any questions I had in mind. He spent nearly three-quarters-of-an-hour answering my questions, which was really quite wonderful – no one else had got this information. Then he sprang it on me, apparently he knew all about me, including my degree at Oxford, and asked if I would like to write his biography. Of course I jumped at the chance, who wouldn't? And then he said something that really threw me a bit off balance – "Come and spend a week with me and we'll see whether we can get on together."

It was therefore with some trepidation that I went back with him to *Parklands*, but Sir Alan was the perfect gentleman. In any case he wasn't interested in me at all. After a few days I fell madly in love with him. He really was the most wonderful person – kind, generous, but he had time for everybody, he was in my view the ideal man – although 16 years older than me that didn't matter. He was the man of my dreams.

However, as I said, he had no interest in me and seemed to have really very little interest in the book I was writing. However, I was fired up and enthusiastic and put my heart and soul into the book.

The more I learnt about Sir Alan, the more I recognised he was a person who had worked hard all his life. He had started in very humble beginnings, but had now reached the epitome, becoming one of the richest men in England. I tried to keep myself apart from the community at *Parklands* and felt that this way I would get a better view of Sir Alan. We had our weekly meetings which did vary, sometimes missing out for as much as three weeks at a time, but he was always courteous and polite and usually gave me as much time as I needed.

Having completed the book I sent it off to various comrades who read it and made corrections and observations, and in the main thought that it was a well researched book. I was delighted when the publisher friend I knew wanted to take the book and I was more than delighted when I was able to tell Sir Alan in answer to his question, "When are you going to get that damn book finished?"
"It is finished."

Two days later after leaving Sir Alan's office, I had a phone call from him. "What are you doing this weekend?" he asked.
"Well, I have nothing organised."
"Right," he said, "I have a meeting in Paris on Saturday morning and after that I am free. Why don't you come with me and we'll celebrate the completion of my book?"
I readily agreed and we flew off on the Friday night, landing at Le Bourgais airport where a car met us. We were taken straight to our hotel, the Westminster Hotel in Rue de la Paix, just off the bottom of the Champs Elysees. It was a beautiful hotel, one apparently where Sir Alan had stayed quite a number of times, and so everyone knew him and received him by name. We had a rather sumptuous dinner, just the two of us. He said to me, "Look I should be back for about 1.00pm tomorrow. Why don't you have a little stroll down Rue de la Paix – after all, it is the centre of the jewellery trade in the whole of Europe, well worth a visit I think."

The next morning after breakfast I was leaving the hotel and the concierge caught up with me. "Miss West," he said "are you going for stroll? Could I suggest that you call in at Cartiers, they are a most prominent jewellers in Paris. If you would like to pass them this card they will certainly treat you well and allow you to see properly anything that you would like to."

"Thank you," I said, so of course I made a beeline for Cartiers. It was only a few doors down from the hotel and I was made very welcome by the jewellers. I spent over an hour being shown beautiful necklaces and rings, and in the end rather nervously I said I wanted to think about it before I purchased. They were very understanding. Things were very expensive there. Despite having saved a lot of money over the last twelve months, I didn't want to spend it all at once.

Sir Alan came back at precisely one o'clock and we had a snack lunch at the hotel. Then he asked if I had been to Paris before. "Yes, I have, as a child, it was a long time ago, but I've never been up the Eiffel Tower."

"Oh good," he said, "Right, let's go up the Eiffel Tower!"

The first thing we did was to catch, one of those open-topped buses which are gorgeous in Spring in Paris. We spent a couple of hours going round on the bus and then being dropped off at the Eiffel Tower. Sir Alan took me right to the top and was pointing out all the different places that you could see. It really was quite a wonderful view, something I had never seen before. He said the most remarkable thing. He said the book was very good and that he had read it completely from beginning to end – in fact, he had done very little else since I had given him a copy. However, he didn't think I should have it printed just yet. He thought there were things to add to it!

"Very good, sir" I said.

"No, no I don't think there is anything missing up until now," he said, "but you know I hope for big events over the next month or so, and I would like these to also be put in the book."

"What's that?" I asked.

"Oh, I can't tell you at the moment, but I will as soon as I can. Look," he said, changing the subject, "I know that I have seemed rather standoffish and not appreciative of your efforts over the last year. I have very much admired the way that you have gone about this book, the whole way in which you have tackled it and you have done an excellent job, but I knew you would."

I didn't know quite what to say.

"Look," he said, "Let's go back to the hotel, I want a rest. Then I have booked a meal on one of the Bateaux Mouches, the boats that sail up and down the Seine, we don't have to be there until eight o'clock."

When they got onto the Bateaux Mouches they had a rather special table. The meal was excellent and it was interesting to cruise down the Seine. Alan seemed rather excited about everything. At the end of the meal he ordered a brandy for each of us. Then he said, "I have something to ask you Sarah. It may come as something of a shock, but I have fallen in love with you. I have been in love with you ever since I saw you at the conference, just over a year ago. I know I haven't been much of a suitor, but I have been, I think, a little embarrassed myself." I gulped. "Do you mind my saying these things?" he continued.

"No not at all, Sir Alan," I replied.

"Do you feel anything for me at all?"

"Yes, I fell in love with you almost immediately after coming to *Parklands*, you are..."

"Oh, will you marry me?"

"Yes," I said "yes".

He produced from his pocket a small box. "This is for you," he said. Inside was the most beautiful rings, one of the ones I had admired so much at Cartiers that morning. I tried it on my finger and it was a perfect fit.

"Oh Alan," I said, "how did you know the size?"

"I know everything about you," he said.

I asked, "When should we get married?"

"That's up to you, but as far as I'm concerned the sooner the better."

"Oh yes, yes," I said.

When we got back to *Parklands* the following day everyone was of course surprised, but they all seemed delighted. They congratulated me and Sir Alan. He said, "I think we ought to go and tell your parents."

So on the Monday morning we shot up to Malvern. We drove up in Alan's car. It was a lovely leisurely drive and we didn't get there until mid-afternoon. My parents were most surprised to see us and then totally over the moon when they heard the news. Mother said, "Oh, we must have time to arrange the wedding," and she started to take over, as I knew she would. Of course the wedding had to be in Malvern and we dashed around all of the next day eventually deciding that it was to be held in August.

August 10th and preparations were hectic and even though there were nearly four months before the wedding it was no time at all. Weddings normally took two years to organise!

The appointed day arrived and the Abbey at Great Malvern was decorated throughout. We had over 350 guests – all my friends from college, from university, mother and father's friends, my aunts and uncles, and then of course everyone from *Parklands* and virtually everyone I can think of from Eden Stanton. The Murrays came from the island, Alan insisted, and even Chantal de Viviers and her daughter Avril. It was a splendid day, the sun shone and at the end of it all I was absolutely worn out – I was shattered. Alan said, "Time for bed dear?" and I replied, "Yes, I think so."

When we went off to bed Alan said, "You can finish the book off now."

If you don't have a dream, how can a dream come true?

EPILOGUE

Alan felt that he would like to add an epilogue to his life story.

I was fortunate to be born to good, caring parents – poor, but they were always encouraging and praising, not only me, but all of the siblings. My father was a real support and always wanted me to, "get ahead in the world," as he put it.

I was fortunate again to get a sponsorship through university, a rare thing in those days. The training I received allowed me to become a leading expert in my field.

My first marriage, whilst ending disastrously, produced two wonderful children who are a complete joy to me and I hold them both very dear in my heart. Despite upsets, they are both hard working, intelligent people and are well set to have successful lives. My second marriage, whilst very new, is I believe a marriage made in heaven. I love Sarah with all my heart and soul. We have not as yet discussed having children, but you never know.

I have met many wonderful people in my life so far. The main catalyst for friendships has been my businesses, but I have always jumped at any opportunity to make friends. I have tried throughout my life to 'have due consideration for other users of life's road', and I have tried to help others who are less fortunate than myself.

My business successes have been a team effort, and I have acted merely as a motivation to a number of clever people.

Two unusual events have dramatically influenced my life. Winning the lottery was of course sheer luck. I was at an extremely low point and I grasped at straws 'to show the world'. Secondly, my belief in dreams and the influence they can have, has taken me on what would seem strange adventures, and usually (but not always) my dreams have been good ones.